No one writes romantic fiction like Barbara Cartland.

Miss Cartland was originally inspired by the best of the romantic novelists she read as a girl —writers such as Elinor Glyn, Ethel M. Dell and E. M. Hull. Convinced that her own wide audience would also delight in her favorite authors, Barbara Cartland has taken their classic tales of romance and specially adapted them for today's readers.

Bantam is proud to publish these novels—personally selected and edited by Miss Cartland—under the imprint

**BARBARA CARTLAND'S
LIBRARY OF LOVE**

Bantam Books by Barbara Cartland
Ask your bookseller for the books you have missed

Barbara Cartland's Library of Love
Leave It to Love
by Pamela Wynne

Condensed by Barbara Cartland

LEAVE IT TO LOVE
A Bantam Book | February 1979

ISBN 0-553-12436-7

Published simultaneously in the United States and Canada

Bantam Books are published by Bantam Books, Inc. Its trademark, consisting of the words "Bantam Books" and the por-
trayal of a bantam, is Registered in U.S. Patent and Trademark
Office and in other countries. Marca Registrada. Bantam
Books, Inc., 666 Fifth Avenue, New York, New York 10019.

PRINTED IN THE UNITED STATES OF AMERICA

Introduction
by
Barbara Cartland

This is a tender, very lovable story which catches at one's heart. I found Gay an irresistible heroine, and her love for the blind Sir Peter was very moving. I longed and longed for the story to end happily.

Chapter
One

Everybody in Woodfield Harmer knew that Miss Fortescue had another companion-help, because everyone always knew what everyone else was doing in that tiny village.

One couldn't help knowing, because it was built like that. One long, rather thin village street, with attractive houses on either side of it.

Woodfield Harmer was so far away from anywhere else that it had never been spoilt.

The Doctor lived in the largest house of all, a house that bulged right onto the street, with no front garden to it, only a strip of grass, edged with white posts from which hung nice solid black chains.

Then came a collection of smaller houses, one of which had converted its parlour into a shop, and there was a nice cheerful glass window full of tins of soup and advertisements for cereal foods.

Miss Fortescue's house was the only ugly

house in the village. She had built it herself, buying a strip of land that the owner of Wally's Farm happened not to want.

It was a thin, red house with two bow windows on either side of the varnished front door, and its windows were always carefully draped with lace curtains.

An ugly flight of stone steps led up to the front door, which opened onto a thin wraith of a hall with a hat-stand and dreadful pictures.

Mrs. Clements, the Vicar's wife, told her husband that it made her feel quite ill to go into Miss Fortescue's house.

"Then try and control it, my dear," said the Vicar, "because Miss Fortescue is uncommonly generous in her subscriptions."

His eyes twinkled.

"I want to get on with the Men's Club this winter. And if the old girl doesn't stump up, because you happen to have offended her, we shall be in the soup."

"Harold, don't be so vulgar, and come and look at Miss Fortescue's new companion-help."

"Where?"

"Coming round from the post-office."

"She looks like you used to," observed the Vicar, standing a little back from the drawing-room window.

"Was I as pretty as that?"

"Much prettier."

"What possessed her to be Miss Fortescue's companion-help?" said Mrs. Clements, her eyes following the slight figure.

"Ask me another!" returned the Vicar. "Probably because she's got to earn her own living and has no qualifications for anything else."

"Couldn't she marry someone?" asked Mrs. Clements dreamily.

"Who?"

"I think she would do for Sir Peter Somerset."

Mrs. Clements turned to her husband.

"I can't endure to think of that young man living all alone in that huge house and cursing Fate and God and everything else. Why can't you make him see you, Harold?"

"My dear child, you can't make a man see you," said the Vicar briefly. "I have called on him twice, as you know."

He sighed.

"But he sees no-one, at least so I understand. I gather he even refuses to call in Dr. Pollard. If he needs a Doctor, he has one down from London."

"Is there not the vaguest hope of him ever getting back his sight?"

"I believe not."

"It's ghastly," said Mrs. Clements heavily. "I saw him the other day in his huge car, and the look on his face as he sat rather huddled in the back of it. It's appalling."

"He must be at least forty, or very near it."

The Vicar paused before he went on:

"It's twenty years since the War, you must remember. And I gather that when he went, he was in his last term at Cambridge. He would have been twenty-one or so then."

"What was he going to be?"

"I don't think he planned to be anything in particular. I believe he was going off big-game shooting or round the world, or something of the kind."

"Harold, they say he drinks most frightfully," said Mrs. Clements dramatically. "And that that valet of his encourages it. I loathe the look of that man; and Sir Peter's never out without him."

"'They say'!" retorted the Vicar. "After all, in a tiny village like this, 'they' say all sorts of things that are not true. You know that quite well."

"Yes, but I believe it is true," replied Mrs. Clements obstinately.

* * *

The Vicar had been right in saying that Gay Hamilton had been obliged to take a post as companion-help because she was not qualified to undertake anything else.

The woman who ran the registry-office in the little country town where Gay had applied for a job had found that out even before the Vicar.

"Previous experience?"

The woman was friendly and not so drastic as most of her compatriots. She eyed Gay over her ledger and even volunteered a smile.

"I . . . I haven't ever done anything before," replied Gay nervously.

"I see."

"But it . . . can't . . . be very difficult to be a house-parlourmaid or housemaid, surely?"

The lady smiled.

4

"More difficult than you think. Also, employers want references. Have you any?"

"No."

"Then . . ."

Miss Bailey laid down her pen.

This was a lady, unmistakably a lady. Well educated; young.

And she had come in by bus from Lewes, instead of trying for a job in the registry-offices there. For there were several registry-offices in Lewes.

That meant that she did not want anyone in her home-town to know that she was taking a job.

Trouble at home? Trouble of her own, of a disreputable kind . . . ?

No. Miss Bailey's profession had taught her to read character. No. This girl with the large, dark eyes was not the type to lose her reputation easily.

Trouble at home? Miss Bailey put it down to that.

"I thought no-one could get servants nowadays," Gay pointed out. "And now that I try to be one, there is no opening for me."

"Would you like me to put your name down on my books?" asked Miss Bailey. "I might get somebody who would be prepared to take an entirely untrained housemaid."

She looked intently at her new client.

"There are such people. Only you must remember that a housemaid works with other servants; would you like that?"

"Should I have a bed-room to myself?"

"Very probably."

"Yes. But then you say that I shall have to wait for a job like that," said Gay, "and I want something at once. Today or tomorrow, for preference."

There was a pause before she added in a low voice:

"I've ... had a row at home. I didn't mean to tell you, but I may as well be frank, or you'll begin to wonder."

Miss Bailey leant back in her chair as Gay continued:

"My mother has ... married again, and my new ... stepfather and I don't hit it off. That's why I didn't go to any of the registry-offices in Lewes. I don't want anyone to know."

"Have you no relations with whom you could go and stay?" asked Miss Bailey kindly.

"No."

"Friends?"

"No. You see, we've always lived more or less abroad," explained Gay. "That is, since Father died.

"He was in the Army, and in marrying again, Mother loses her pension. I get a little, about fifty pounds a year I think it is, but it won't keep me.

"So Mother is entirely dependent on my stepfather, who detests me and wants me ... out of the way. They get on fairly well, in fact very well, if I'm not there. So I am determined to get away.

"If I go to stay with relations or friends, it only means that I've got to go back again. I want to cut right away for good.

"Haven't you *anything*?" ended Gay in a

flood of disappointment as she leant on the top of the shabby desk.

"Yes, I have one intensely disagreeable job on my books," said Miss Bailey frankly.

She leant back in her chair and surveyed Gay dispassionately.

"There is a Miss Fortescue, who lives in a village about twenty-five miles from here, a village called Woodfield Harmer."

Gay brightened visibly as Miss Bailey went on:

"It has no station of its own, but a bus stops about half-a-mile away from it, a bus that goes to Brighton.

"Miss Fortescue is so well known that hardly any registry-office will help her. I put her on my books because I used to know her brother very well," said Miss Bailey briefly.

"Yes, go on, please."

"I don't know why I am telling you, but I was once engaged to him."

Miss Bailey's nice steady gaze flickered a little.

"Oh! Were you?"

"Yes, and then he died," Miss Bailey added simply, and she bent her eyes to her ledger and sat very still.

"Oh! I am sorry."

And then there was a little silence, finally broken by Miss Bailey.

"I have told you this in confidence."

Gay smiled gently.

"Of course."

So this elderly spinster lady had had a love-affair. And the man had died. Just that one flash of romance that had ended in nothing, and yet it had kept her sweet and charitable.

"Tell me more about Miss Fortescue's job," she pleaded. "And for what position does she want someone? Could I do it, do you suppose?"

"Can you cook at all?"

"I could in a pinch," said Gay. "In fact, I could do anything in a pinch, I am so mad keen to get away from home. Tell me about the job, will you?"

So Miss Bailey went into details. Miss Fortescue wanted a companion-help, she explained, which meant that Gay would live in the house as Miss Fortescue's equal.

She would have to do housework, lay the table, and do the shopping, and if there was a dog, take it for a walk.

She would not have to cook unless the woman who came in by the day failed to arrive.

"But I warn you that Miss Fortescue is not easy to live with," Miss Bailey pointed out. "To my certain knowledge, she has had three companion-helps already this year, and Heaven knows how many last year."

"Are they easy to get then?"

"They are rather."

"All the same, I think I shall go." Gay smiled faintly. "How much salary does Miss Fortescue pay?"

"Thirty-five pounds a year."

"Isn't that rather a little?"

"Yes, it's more than rather a little, it is a very little," said Miss Bailey drily. "But it's all she will give; and of course when you reckon in board and lodging and washing, it comes to more."

"I see. When does she want someone?" asked Gay.

"At once."

"Could I start tomorrow?"

"Yes, certainly tomorrow. If I write this morning, she will get it this afternoon. As a matter of fact, I think I could arrange a lift for you into Woodfield Harmer tomorrow afternoon."

"How extremely kind of you," said Gay warmly.

"Well, I don't really know that I am helping you in sending you to Miss Fortescue. I believe she is extremely unpleasant to work for. However . . ."

"Was Mr. Fortescue like her?" asked Gay naïvely.

"Not in the least," replied Miss Bailey, and her eyes softened in laughter as she glanced at the young face before her.

What this young creature wanted was a kind husband to love and look after her, thought Miss Bailey, rapidly jotting things down in a large ledger.

Love . . . and all the things that she herself had missed, she thought dispassionately, wondering subconsciously how this girl was going to break it to her mother that she was leaving home for good. . . .

* * *

Miss Fortescue had the knack of making everyone who worked for her wretched.

9

The woman who came in by the day to cook hated her and said so openly.

"You won't stick it for long!"

Her tone was emphatic as she banged about the kitchen.

"And I wouldn't, only my husband's been out of work for so long and it's difficult for me to get anything now that the winter's coming on."

She snorted.

"Nasty old busybody she is, and I'll tell her so before I've done with her."

Gay, with a look of dignity on her expressive mouth, went upstairs with the can of hot water she had come to fetch.

For there was no hot water in the bath-room. She had found that out the night before, when she had hopefully remarked that as she would rather like a bath, she would go to bed early.

"A bath?"

Miss Fortescue's beady eyes had narrowed as she sat on one side of the minute fire, playing Patience.

"Yes, a bath. Why, isn't it convenient?" asked Gay calmly.

For although she had been in the house only five hours, she knew that she was going to hate it. It was an ugly, mean little house. In the sitting-room were dreadful photographs of Miss Fortescue's relations.

Only one looked at all nice: a man in a frock coat, with his hand thrust into his waistcoat. That must be the one who had been engaged to Miss Bailey, reflected Gay, staring at it.

"You can have a bath on Saturday, if you

either light the copper yourself or get Mrs. Walters to do it," returned Miss Fortescue, turning up cards very rapidly.

"And will you please see that my hot-water bottle is placed in my bed and that it is hot, and that my bed is turned down and the curtains are drawn."

Gay stood up, and her dark eyes remained expressionless as Miss Fortescue went on:

"And as I always have a cup of hot milk and Ovaltine at ten o'clock, you cannot go to bed before that hour, as you will of course make it.

"And do put the tray ready for my early tea; I require it punctually at half-past seven in the morning. You get up early, I hope, as I like to come down to a nice bright fire in this room.

"There is a gas fire in the dining-room. Mrs. Walters gets here in time to prepare breakfast, at least I hope she does, as I daresay you are not a very experienced cook."

She gestured to Gay impatiently.

"Now, sit down again, please, as your standing about makes me feel restless and uncertain. Get a book and read it. There is no need for you to move about until half-past nine, as I like my hot-water bottle to be really hot. Don't you play Patience?"

"No," replied Gay.

She sat down again and felt a sudden unaccustomed inclination to tears.

"I must teach you Poker-Patience," said Miss Fortescue briskly.

Her beady eyes darted over the neat rows of cards.

"I like my companion-help to be busy in some way or another. Perhaps you knit?"

"Not very well," said Gay lamely.

"You crochet, then?"

"No; I'm not very much good at any sort of needlework," said Gay. "I don't know why. I never seem to have had much time for it."

"Indeed!"

"My mother and I lived almost entirely abroad," explained Gay, feeling a sudden longing to speak of her home.

Not that it was home to her any more, but it did contain her mother, after all.

"Indeed," said Miss Fortescue again, showing by every line of her hard little face that she was not in the least interested.

"Yes," answered Gay, who, now that the fire had burnt through a little, was feeling better because her feet were warm.

"Have you been abroad?" she asked conversationally.

"What I have or have not done is not a matter that I care to discuss with my companion-help," said Miss Fortescue acidly.

"Kindly occupy yourself with a book until it is time to get my hot-water bottle. You will find books on the shelf by the window, but do not remove them from this room, please."

A quick retort trembled on Gay's tongue, but she bit it back.

This was only the first day with this dreadful, withered old maid; in fact it wasn't really a day, it was only five hours that she had been there.

Five hours; and she was obliged by law to

stay for a month, unless she cared to forego her wages.

And if she went, where would she go?

Gay stood up and walked over to the book-shelf. Her slender hands were clenched by her sides and her delicate face was scarlet.

This, then, was what it was to have to earn a living! To put up with everything that one's employer chose to say or do. If only she could cook well, in which case she would be so valuable that no-one would dare to be rude to her!

No wonder women went into shops and offices, where they were not dependent on the whims, tempers, and meannesses of other women, thought Gay, standing with her back to Miss Fortescue and trembling with misery and fatigue.

And now she could not go to bed for an hour because of the Ovaltine.

She put out a shaking hand and took a book at random.

"Which book have you chosen?"

"Well . . . it's a very heavy one," said Gay tremulously.

Lifting it, she smiled feebly.

Gay turned to see Miss Fortescue's beady eyes fixed on her.

"The *Stores Catalogue*," she said. "Ten years old. That will be interesting, as I was ten then."

She made an effort at conversation, as she went on:

"I used to like the pictures, and once I stayed with an aunt near Cambridge and she used to let me cut them out with very blunt scissors."

13

"Indeed."

Gay returned to her chair and wondered what would happen when the fire needed some more coal, as the coal-scuttle was empty. In half-an-hour the fire would have got quite low.

She sat very still, the heavy book on her knee, and wondered if it would be possible in the future for her to spend her evenings in the kitchen. . . .

* * *

The next morning Gay awoke with a start.

Someone in the house was already awake, for there were sounds of raking and banging in the kitchen below her. But what was there to rake? The water had run cold in the taps last night; hot at first, and then cold.

And who could be in the kitchen? Had she overslept? She glanced hurriedly at her travelling-clock standing dejectedly on the bamboo table by her side. No, it was only half-past seven.

Getting out of bed and shivering at the touch of the floor-matting on her bare feet, she ran to the wash-hand stand and brushed her teeth and sponged her face in cold water.

She would put on one of her new overalls, gay and starred with roses.

If Miss Fortescue didn't like it, she could do the other thing, thought Gay, refreshed from her good night's sleep and feeling young and adventurous again.

She smiled and her pale face dimpled and her dark eyes shone as she ran downstairs and opened the kitchen door.

She was determined to be agreeable whatever happened. After all, Miss Fortescue might be one of those people who softened if you were nice to them.

"Good-morning, Miss."

It was Mrs. Walters, in a man's cap, sweeping out the kitchen with vigour.

"Oh, I thought you didn't come till much later," Gay said with a smile, feeling a wave of relief sweep over her.

"Nor do I. But I knew how the old girl was carrying on. I've lived with her off and on a good few years. And she daren't part with me, because I know her too well and I do her cooking, and she likes her food," said Mrs. Walters, winking.

She leant casually on her broom-handle.

"I've seen a good score of you young ladies come and go this last year! Not that they were like you, because they weren't, they weren't real ladies; and some I told so, too, when they got a bit uppish!"

She chuckled.

"But you're different. And I've come here early today to light the boiler because it's not fair that you should stick in a place where there's no hot water."

Gay smiled at Mrs. Walters as she went on:

"Hark at it roaring; that'll bring the old girl down unless I'm very much mistaken," said Mrs. Walters maliciously.

"Yes, but . . ."

"You leave her to me, Miss," ordered Mrs. Walters. "Here she comes, curl-papers and boudoir-cap and all."

15

"Ah! Mrs. Walters!"

The two women were staring at each other, Mrs. Walters leaning on her broom with exaggerated ease.

"I see that you have lit the boiler."

"Yes, of course I have."

Mrs. Walters began to sweep rather noisily again.

"You don't suppose that a young lady like this is going to stay in a poky, nasty little house like this without any hot water to wash in, do you? Now you get along back upstairs where you belong at this hour and leave us to get on with our work. Hurry along now!"

"Mrs. Walters!"

"Get along with you!"

Mrs. Walters took a threatening step forward, and at the same time wrenched off the top of the boiler and stared at the glowing, roaring contents of it.

And to Gay's amazement, Miss Fortescue went.

She herself was very slightly trembling, she found, gripping her hands together in impatience and hoping that Mrs. Walters had not noticed.

"However dared you?" she asked.

"Dared! It's her that daren't," said Mrs. Walters, sniffing. "Liver and bacon today, and pancakes, and she's looking forward to them, too. Loves her food, she does!"

She reached up for a willow-patterned teapot.

"And now, if you'd like to sit down over

there by the fire, I'll make you a nice cup of tea, and then have my own when you've gone to dust the drawing-room."

Gay obediently sat down, and thrust her slender hands into the pockets of her overalls.

"Do you take sugar, Miss?" asked Mrs. Walters, now busy in the larder.

"Yes, please."

"And now, if I might make so bold as to ask, what made a pretty young lady like you take a nasty job like this?" enquired Mrs. Walters, sitting back comfortably in her chair.

As Gay looked at her, her young heart flooded out in gratitude to the motherly woman who had shown her such kindness.

"My mother married again, and my stepfather didn't want me at home," said Gay frankly. "I didn't want to stay there and spoil everything for Mother."

She smiled faintly.

"As I wanted to get away at once and am absolutely untrained, I took the first thing I could get."

"Which was this?"

Gay nodded, her eyes dancing. For somehow everything seemed different now and she felt happier than she had in weeks.

In fact, ever since that loathsome day when her mother had told her that she was going to be married again and that they would all live together in the little house at Lewes and be as happy as crickets.

"And how long do you suppose you'll be able

17

to stick with it?" enquired Mrs. Walters derisively, drinking her tea as her bright eyes surveyed Gay over the rim of her cup.

"For months, so long as you're here," said Gay confidently.

Somehow she knew that in Mrs. Walters she had found a friend.

Even the hateful evenings could be borne, with the prospect of a nice, cheerful early-morning tea-party like the one they were having now.

"Yes, but I don't always come early like this," Mrs. Walters pointed out, getting up from the table and going over to the cupboard.

"Although I don't know that I won't, now that the winter's drawing in, for my husband doesn't go to work so early as he does in the summer."

Her eyes twinkled mischievously.

"So I'll tell the old girl that I want an extra five shillings or so to come and light the boiler in the mornings. Twenty-five shillings a week, that'll be," said Mrs. Walters sagely.

"Good heavens! And she only gives me thirty-five pounds a year," said Gay.

"That's because young ladies like you will take it," observed Mrs. Walters. "We won't, and that's where we score.

"And now the tray for the old girl, and her tea-pot and the cosy and all the set-out that she likes."

And Gay, standing there, watched Mrs. Walters getting it all ready. It was only five to eight, and yet she felt as if she had been up for hours!

She must do some work: sweep the sitting-

18

room and dust it, and make her own bed and tidy her hideous little bed-room.

"And now, Miss, take my tip and don't stand any back-chat from the old girl," admonished Mrs. Walters. "Give her her tea and then just leave her to it and get on with your job."

Mrs. Walters watched Gay walk across the tiny hall and up the stairs, her slim ankles neat in their silk stockings.

"A thousand pities," she said with a sigh, speaking half-aloud as she went back into the kitchen. "What that young lady wants is a nice husband to take care of her, not to come and take a job like this."

Gay stood by the narrow bed and listened to her employer's acid commentary on the woman who had routed her.

"But I never bandy words with the lower classes," she said crisply. "Mrs. Walters does her work efficiently and well, and that is enough for me.

"Kindly close the door quietly when you go out, Miss Hamilton."

Chapter
Two

Woodfield Harmer possessed only one large house, and that was Simon's Close, which stood all by itself on a little hill overlooking the river.

Behind it, the trees came up close and seemed to stand sentinel over the mullioned windows and old cobbled courtyard.

The former coach-house was now a garage, where the long, dust-coloured Chrysler stretched its lines and almost seemed to yawn with boredom at the silence that brooded over the old house.

A silence that was broken only by the cawing of rooks as they rustled and chattered in the tall elms. Or by the sound of the wind as it swept up the estuary and stirred the long branches so that they swayed and danced and sent long, flickering shadows over the old grey house.

But now, for a wonder, there was the sound of voices in the huge paved hall.

Miss Mannering, who came every morning to

read to Sir Peter, had been given the sack and was complaining bitterly about it to the house-keeper.

She stood there with tears streaming down her sallow cheeks.

"I have never been spoken to like that in the whole of my life!" she wailed. "Sir Peter was positively insulting, and after I've come here in all weathers every day for weeks!"

She paused to blow her nose loudly before she went on:

" 'You've got a voice like a file,' he said, 'it makes me sick, sick, I tell you. I'll give you twice your salary to clear out at once, this instant.' "

"I'm very sorry," said the housekeeper apologetically. "But when Sir Peter gets into these states, we can do nothing but leave him entirely alone. I am very sorry, I am sure, Miss Mannering."

"It's not your fault, Mrs. James."

"No, I know, but— Ah, here is Mr. Fenton with your salary," said Mrs. James suddenly, as a slim figure came sliding down the wide stair-case; a slim figure that seemed to have appeared from nowhere.

And how had Mrs. James seen him? wondered Miss Mannering, for she had never turned her head. Really, she would be glad to get out of this house, she thought uneasily.

All so strange, and the smell of spirits in Sir Peter's study, a smell such as one got when the door of a public-house swung open.

And yet the dignity of Sir Peter's tall lean figure, with the bright, piercing blue eyes that looked as if they could see through and through

21

you, although they really couldn't see anything at all.

The beauty of the vast, high-ceilinged room with the walls all lined with books.

And the glorious fires, for somehow Sir Peter always seemed to be cold; he would sit near the fire with his hand on his spaniel's neck, and stare, or appear to be staring, into the flames.

Yes, there was plenty of money about, thought Miss Mannering enviously, for she was poor and lived with her widowed mother.

And the two pounds a week had been a help, for it was very generous pay. Two pounds a week for reading to someone for three hours a day, either in the morning or the afternoon, as Sir Peter wished.

Yes, it was going to be a loss, thought Miss Mannering, her thin nose turning a little pink at the tip at the thought of the loss that it was going to be.

"Here is your cheque, Miss Mannering."

Mr. Fenton, the valet-secretary, had arrived in the hall.

"And Sir Peter wished to give you a whole month's salary, as the engagement has terminated without notice."

"Oh, thank you very much indeed!"

The relief was so great that Miss Mannering almost cried out the words.

Nine pounds, and Christmas was coming! Why, it was a small fortune. She was even able to smile at Mr. Fenton, whom she detested.

But Mr. Fenton had already started to go up the stairs again. Wonderful stairs, branching out like the arms of a candelabrum. And high walls hung with old oil paintings.

The thin, dark figure looked like a shadow on the stairs. A horrid shadow, a shadow that slanted sideways, grotesque, distorted.

Somehow Miss Mannering could not stop looking at it. There! It had gone, leaving almost a physical sensation of its presence.... Miss Mannering came to herself with a jerk.

"It is most generous of Sir Peter," she murmured.

"I am so glad," said Mrs. James softly.

Mrs. James was a real lady, thought Miss Mannering, and yet she was so afraid of Mr. Fenton. One would think that she would be able to tackle a nasty fellow like that.

It was just as if Mr. Fenton had the whole house in the hollow of his hand. The servants were all afraid of him too. The chauffeur took his orders from Mr. Fenton, and so did the butler.

The new butler, that was; the old one, who had been with the family for years, had left the year before.

Turned out, so the village said, because he spoke up about the way Sir Peter drank and about the way Mr. Fenton encouraged it.

"Well, I had better be going," said Miss Mannering, feeling quite sure that it was of no use at all to say anything to Mrs. James about the way things were going at Simon's Close.

After all, there was always a chance that she might be back again. People who could read aloud were few and far between in Woodfield Harmer.

And in the meantime she had a cheque for nine pounds in her suede bag. She would change it at the bank on the way home and buy a grapefruit for her mother.

There was something so grand about a grapefruit, thought Miss Mannering, taking Mrs. James's outstretched hand.

*   *   *

In spite of Mrs. Walters' kindness to her, Gay very soon began to get a feeling that if she stayed even a month at Miss Fortescue's, she would die before she got to the end of it.

There was something so awful about it, so ghastly. And yet what was there that was really awful?

The food was plentiful and now the water was always hot. Mrs. Walters had insisted on the boiler being kept going night and day.

"And I'll come earlier to see to it," she informed Miss Fortescue. "You'll have to pay me extra for it, but you can well afford it, Miss, and that I know very well."

And Miss Fortescue, with her usual docility where Mrs. Walters was concerned, gave in.

And if Gay had known it, never had a companion-help had such a time!

Yet the dreary primness of the little house seemed to close in on her like a sort of awful fog. The evenings . . . the despair of the evenings.

"I really feel that if I have another evening here, I shall die!"

Gay, sitting down very hard on a kitchen chair, said the words forcibly to Mrs. Walters.

"What's the matter with the evenings then?"

"That room . . . and the tiny little fire that I have to huddle over if I am to feel any heat at all. And knowing that I have to wait up to get her Ovaltine and her hot-water bottle."

Gay sighed heavily.

Mrs. Walters, peeling potatoes, looked up to survey the slim girl, and there was a whimsical twist to the corners of her mouth.

"You've got to choke all that down when you earn your own living," said Mrs. Walters wisely.

"I can't."

"Then don't earn your own living! It's a waste of your own time and everyone else's."

She paused before she continued gently:

"Go home and live the sort of life that other young ladies of your age live. Chance her not giving you your week's wage, and clear out."

"I tell you, I can't go home," said Gay.

She turned to face Mrs. Walters.

"I've told you about my stepfather. They don't want me at home, and I'm not trained for any kind of decent job. What shall I do?"

In her delicate face, her blue eyes were strained and almost desperate.

"Stick with this position," answered Mrs. Walters sensibly, reaching to get the matches down from the mantlepiece preparatory to lighting one of the jets of the gas stove.

"I can't."

"I'll make up a good fire in the sitting-room before I go. Then you'll be warm, and I know that means a lot to you."

"She follows me into the kitchen when I go to

25

fill her hot-water bottle," said Gay. "I hear her coming in her felt slippers and I get a feeling as if she were coming to murder me."

She shuddered.

"I can't explain it. It's something in this house. . . . I believe it's haunted!" she said with a gasp.

"Haunted!" scoffed Mrs. Walters. "Not a bit of it. It's you. It's your nerves, Miss. Get out more. You've been here a week, haven't you? Well, go out this afternoon."

"Oh, no, I should hate it," said Gay instantly. "Besides, if I go out I've got to come back. And she would never let me go, and I certainly couldn't ask her."

"I could, though," said Mrs. Walters with decision.

* * *

After making up her mind to go and see Miss Fortescue that afternoon, Mrs. Clements suddenly said that she couldn't.

"And why not?" enquired the Vicar amiably, for the Vicar was used to his wife's sudden change of front.

"I feel that if I saw that pretty, graceful girl looking miserable, I should want to take her away from Miss Fortescue's and mother her," replied Mrs. Clements.

"And I couldn't possibly do it, because of all the things she subscribes to, as well as for lots of other reasons. Don't you agree?"

"Entirely," said the Vicar thankfully. "Let's

go for a good walk instead. We'll call in at the
post-office on our way."

And it was in the post-office that they met
Gay. Mrs. Clements saw her first.

"There she is."

She touched the Vicar's arm.

"Who?" asked the Vicar, with a little inner
groan, for he had hoped to get out of the Parish
without being buttonholed by some woman or
other.

"Miss Fortescue's companion-help. I'm going
to speak to her."

Gay would not have believed it possible that
in one short half-hour she could feel so different.

Out of range of the ugly little house next to
Wally's Farm, she felt all her sense of adventure
surging up again.

Six hours all to herself, for Miss Fortescue
had told her that she need not be back until half-
past seven. Well, in six hours anything might happen.

And after buying her stamps, she had decided to catch the bus to Brighton. It meant a little walk towards Selmeston, so Mrs. Walters had
told her, but Gay didn't mind that, and the bus
ran to Brighton every half-hour and it took thirty-
five minutes to get there.

She would have plenty of time to have tea
there and look at the shops and perhaps go on the
pier.

Gay turned from the post-office counter to
meet Mrs. Clements' nice frank smile.

"I'm sure you won't mind my speaking to you

without an introduction," said Mrs. Clements pleasantly.

And then she explained who she was and why she had spoken to Gay.

Gay answered in her low, rather husky voice, and Mrs. Clements, hearing it, wondered what on earth had possessed this girl to take a job with Miss Fortescue. For her face was delicate and distinguished, and her voice . . .

"Harry!"

Mrs. Clements turned to call to her husband. "One moment."

The Vicar was talking to someone who had just come into the post-office.

Someone tall, with a grey felt hat dragged down very low over his eyes. Someone who groped, thought Gay, watching the man with eyes suddenly gone bright with interest.

Not blind, surely, that magnificent-looking man with the tragic mouth.

Oh no! He had lifted his head and was looking straight at her. . . .

He and the Vicar were coming towards them. Ah . . . yes, he was blind!

How too awful, thought Gay, watching with swift, almost tormenting compassion the way in which the tall man laid a groping hand on the Vicar's arm.

"Cynthia, Sir Peter would like to speak to you."

The Vicar had come to a standstill.

"You know my wife, of course."

"How do you do."

Now the tall man's head was bared and Gay

28

could see the dark hair tinged with grey at the temples.

"How do you do, Sir Peter."

Mrs. Clements had a charming and very cordial way of speaking, and she took the outstretched hand very closely in hers.

"And now I have a friend here beside me whom you do not know, nor does my husband know her either," said Mrs. Clements, smiling up into the sightless eyes. "Miss Gay Hamilton, isn't it?"

"Yes," answered Gay shyly.

The sight of this blind man had upset her in some queer, unaccountable way.

How too awful to be blind like that. And to be quite young as well.

What did he do with himself all the time and how could he bear it?

He couldn't bear it, one could tell that by the look on his mouth. It was a stricken mouth, a bitter mouth.

The whole of him was bitter. And he was untidy and his hat wanted brushing, thought Gay.

"Can't I take you for a run in the car?"

Sir Peter was talking to the Vicar.

"And perhaps Miss Hamilton?"

Gay could have sworn that the keen blue eyes were looking her through and through. . . .

"Oh no, thank you very much. I have one or two things that I must do."

Shyly Gay excused herself. Yes, she said, she would call at the Vicarage, she would love to. And then she made her way out of the post-office.

Ah, that must be Sir Peter's car, she thought, surveying the long saloon drawn close up to the kerb with a chauffeur and a man sitting beside him. The man turned and stared at her rather rudely, Gay felt, as she hunted for the letter-box.

"Yes, I'd better go and see what he's up to."

The man was speaking to the chauffeur. But surely he was not speaking about Sir Peter Somerset, thought Gay, suddenly feeling angry and up in arms as the man got out onto the pavement.

"There's the letter-box, Miss."

Mr. Fenton's voice and smile were ingratiating.

"Thank you." Gay's voice was frigid.

She would hurry away before they came out of the post-office, she decided, and also get out of range of this hateful, slimy-looking creature who was staring at her.

Who could he be to speak so familiarly of Sir Peter to a servant? wondered Gay, feeling her resentment disappear as the soft sunshine lay across her hat.

It was a divine afternoon for a walk, and Brighton would be such fun.

Woodfield Harmer was most awfully pretty, thought Gay, staring about her. Lovely woods and fields. A signpost pointed over a field: RIGHT-OF-WAY TO SELMESTON. Yes, that was obviously the way one had to go to catch the bus.

But she was quite halfway across the second field before Mr. Fenton caught her up.

He was in a vile temper, for Sir Peter had told him curtly that he was taking Mr. and Mrs.

Clements for a drive and therefore he had better go back to Simon's Close on foot.

Mr. Fenton was not used to being told to go anywhere on foot. For some time now he had got out of the habit of taking orders.

Also, he disliked Bennett, the chauffeur, seeing him in such a position. However . . .

"Certainly, Sir," he said urbanely.

As soon as the car was out of sight, he started in pursuit of Gay. A visitor to Woodfield Harmer, of course. Such a hold of a place could not produce anything as good-looking as that.

In five minutes or so he was abreast of her.

"Good-afternoon, Miss," he said, lifting his hat.

And Gay, who had heard footsteps behind her, suddenly felt sick with fright. The same revolting man who had got out of the car and stared at her!

Who could he be? Not a gentleman, of course, one could tell that by his voice. And he had followed her. What for? wondered Gay, her heart beating rapidly.

"Good-afternoon," she said coolly.

She slackened her speed a little so that he could pass her on the narrow path.

"Going for a walk?"

"Yes, but not with you."

Gay's courage rose with her anger.

"Please either go on or go back, but whichever way you go, stop being impertinent to me."

"Hoity-toity," mocked Mr. Fenton.

He put out a quick arm to encircle her waist.

31

"Come come, you're a pretty little creature, but pretty little creatures like you shouldn't scratch."

"Let go of me!" cried Gay.

She suddenly felt sick and faint with terror, because here she was entirely at the mercy of this ghastly man.

Memories of her early girlhood fled over her.

This man had the same sort of face as the men who used to hang about the Common near her home. Men who weren't men at all, but infinitely lower than animals.

"Come come," cajoled Mr. Fenton, who was beginning to enjoy himself.

This girl was young and fragrant and, for the moment anyway, in his power.

And Mr. Fenton loved having people in his power. It gave him quite a peculiar thrill, he thought, pursing up his lips.

"Let me go," pleaded Gay, fighting and slipping on the wet grass by the side of the path.

"Not without a kiss," said Mr. Fenton, breathing heavily.

Gay was strong, and he was distinctly flabby.

"Not without a kiss," he repeated fatuously.

And then, with a start, he almost flung her from him.

Someone was coming, curse them! A couple of labourers were stepping leisurely over a hedge leading out of a little copse ahead of them.

"Oh!"

And now Gay was running towards them.

"Please, please!" she cried as they stared with round eyes at her. "That man!"

"Which man?"

They stared curiously past her at the retreating figure.

"It's Fenton from Simon's Close," remarked the elder of the two, shrugging his shoulders.

"That's all right, Miss," he assured her. "He's off. Walking to Selmeston, were you? Carry on, Miss, you're safe enough now."

"He might come back."

"Not he, with us behind him," said the younger man, grinning. "Were you going to catch the bus to Brighton? You'll just do it if you hurry."

"Somehow now I don't feel as if I could."

Gay stood there, her soft mouth trembling.

"I'm not generally so stupid as this," she went on, "but . . . he . . . gave me the most awful fright."

"We'll see you to the bus," the elder of the men offered kindly. "It's only just across the next field, and we can go home that way, can't we, George?"

"That's right," replied George accommodatingly.

"Oh, but I don't like to take you out of your way."

Gay's large eyes were anxious.

"And then when I come back, I shall have to come this way alone. I don't believe I could now," she added tremulously.

"When are you coming back, Miss?"

"At about six."

"Then you'll find a pack of Woodfield Harmer folk on the bus," said the elder of the two men. "And Fenton'll not be trying any of his tricks with them about. Come along, Miss, or you'll miss the three-o'clock bus."

How kind they were, thought Gay, her spirits going up again with a leap as they went across the field.

She wanted to get right away, into something new, so that for at least a few hours she could forget Miss Fortescue and the sombre little house where she had to live.

"I can't thank you enough," she said fervently as they reached the little wooden shelter that was the bus-stop.

"Don't mention it, Miss."

Both men smiled and touched their caps and were gone. As they walked away, they spoke of the man who had frightened this pretty young creature.

"Wants a good horsewhipping," muttered the elder of the two.

"And he's not likely to get that," observed George, feeling in his pocket for his packet of cigarettes.

"Our Jim's been taken on at the Close to help the gardener, and he says that Fenton runs the place, gives the orders and pays the bills, and makes himself a so-and-so nuisance all round."

He paused for a moment to light his cigarette, then he went on:

"And, Jim says, Sir Peter never does a thing except get tight."

"A pity," said his companion, sighing. "Ought not to be possible for a gentleman like Sir Peter to get into that state, and with all the money he's got, too."

"But can't anything be done about his blindness? They do such marvels nowadays," said George.

The elder man thought for a moment.

"How old is he? Can't be much more than thirty-eight or so. Went to the War straight from college, so they tell me."

"Yes, that's right," agreed George. "And I think he's seen all the Doctors that there are."

He shook his head slowly.

"Hopeless, they say it is. Optic-nerve gone, or something. Sight just winked out after an explosion. Black as night all of a sudden. Enough to upset any man, that would be."

"That's right," said the elder man, nodding.

And he went off towards home thinking of Gay's pale, terrified young face, and of the man who had caused that terror.

Living on the fat of the land and swindling his employer in the bargain, not to mention encouraging him to drink all day, reflected the elder man, who knew a great deal more about the household at Simon's Close than George did.

*   *   *

Gay thoroughly enjoyed the afternoon at Brighton. She went swinging along, her delicate face all aglow with pleasure and excitement.

For all of a sudden life had become an adventure again. Anything might happen. Gay felt suddenly sure of it. The horrid little house where she was earning her living was only an interlude.

This was life: Brighton with its gay shops and crowded streets and brilliantly lit Parade.

Part of the way home lay along the Parade and by now it would all be lit up. All those huge, wonderful hotels lit up, thought Gay. It would be an adventure in itself to see them.

The journey home was delightful. The omnibus took on the colours of the myriad electric lights on the Parade, and slid along as a transformed thing.

A fairy-coach, thought Gay, who felt perfectly happy because she heard several people asking for tickets for Woodfield Harmer.

That meant that she would have company across the fields, so there was nothing to be afraid of. And it made the thought of coming to Brighton again very much nicer.

Every week she would come, decided Gay, hugging her bag close up to her side.

Mrs. Walters had said that she was entitled to an afternoon and evening out once a week if not twice, so next time she would stay out very much longer.

Miss Fortescue would soon get used to it, reflected Gay, and it was much better not to give in to her, because Mrs. Walters got her own way entirely by simply saying that she was going to do a thing and then doing it.

The way back across the fields held no terrors this time, for it was simply a stream of chattering men and girls all on their way home after work in Brighton.

Gay followed behind them as they swung along with linked arms. They apparently all knew one another and were on excellent terms with the bus-conductor, for they whistled and waved to him as the long, silent streak of the omnibus, a blaze of light, went sliding away down the hill.

She went over the stile and then was in the village street. A friendly street, decided Gay, with twinkling lights in some of the windows.

She walked slowly, enjoying the crisp, frosty feeling in the air.

There were bright lights in the windows of the little inn at the corner.

It was a famous inn and had been an old posting-house. Henry VIII had once stopped there on his way to London, so Mrs. Walters had said.

Gay decided to stop and have a good look at it. There was an inscription over the door, only it was too dark to see it.

She went up close to see if she could decipher it. Yes, she could just see the date, but it was in Roman letters.

And then she jumped back. Someone was coming out of the inn; someone tall, who was unsteady on his feet.

How too awful for words. Someone drunk. She shrank back into the shadows.

"Bennett!"

The figure had stopped dead and was calling out:

"Bennett! Bennett, where are you? Blast you!"

"Can I do anything?"

37

In an instant, Gay had grasped that it was Sir Peter Somerset. He was expecting his car to be there, but it wasn't.

"Can I do anything?" she asked again, and her voice was steady.

"Who are you?"

Yes, he was undoubtedly drunk, decided Gay, watching his hesitating movements. And yet somehow she was not in the least afraid.

"I met you in the post-office," she replied quietly. "You were with the Vicar. Do you remember?"

"Oh yes, the girl with the golden voice," said Sir Peter.

He dragged off his soft hat.

"Of course; and now I'm in the soup, girl with the golden voice. My chauffeur has not come back for me as I told him to. Where the hell do you suppose he is?"

"I haven't the least idea. What else could he be doing, do you suppose?"

"He might have mistaken what I said and have gone on to the Forge," replied Sir Peter.

He swayed slightly.

"But the point is that it's a little difficult for me to get about alone. I'm blind, girl with the golden voice. Blind as the proverbial bat."

He turned his face towards her.

"How would you like to be blind, my child? To have to stand still and wait for some kind person to come and lead you about? Jolly, isn't it?"

"I am not at all sure that it wouldn't be worse to be absolutely stone deaf."

In the darkness, she went up close to the tall man swaying unsteadily on his feet and slipped her arm through his.

"I'll take you anywhere you want to go," she offered quietly.

And as she stood there she felt as if her heart had melted in her body for sheer pity.

No wonder he drank. Who wouldn't drink if it made them forget for a minute or two their terrible plight?

And supposing he was drunk; what did she care? To see him there in the dark, towering over her and yet as helpless as a baby. More helpless, really, than a baby.

"It's extremely kind of you," said Sir Peter, and now he spoke a little indistinctly.

"But I think you ought to know that I am more than a little drunk. I am one of those unfortunate people who are aware of it, you see."

"Please take my arm," said Gay urgently.

She was suddenly conscious that the only feeling she had at that moment was that no-one must see this man as he was then.

The shame of it! Sir Peter Somerset coming out of a local inn, drunk.

"I repeat that it is extremely kind of you," said Sir Peter.

Leaning rather heavily on her arm, he took a few uncertain steps.

They turned their backs on the little inn, the light of it flooding out behind them, showing his long shadow looming over hers.

"Do we turn to the left or right?" he asked, and now his voice was steady again.

He had a charming, cultured voice, thought Gay, pressing a little on his arm to guide him. "The left."

"Thank you."

"I love a street like this in the dark," said Gay simply. "I will tell you what it's like."

She lifted her face, pausing for a moment before she went on:

"Against the sky, because the moon is getting up, you can see the uneven roofs of houses, and behind some of them are trees that look rather as if they were cut out of black paper; you know—they show jagged against the sky.

"Some of the windows are lighted up, and now we are passing one that is."

"And what can you see inside?"

"Someone sewing. A woman. She has a lamp on the table . . . and now she has leant forward to turn it up a little."

"Go on."

"The house that we are passing now has the curtains drawn."

"Tiresome people."

"Yes; and I always wish they would leave the curtains open so that one could see in. Now here is one that has. Let us stop for a second, shall we?"

"By all means. What can you see?"

"People having tea. Under a lamp without any shade. Five of them. It's an ugly room with dark wallpaper."

"Displeasing?"

"Very!"

"How near are we to the village shops?" asked

40

Sir Peter. "I know the village well, so that gives
me a clue."

"I can see the windows of the greengrocer's."

"Oh yes, I remember."

"And now I rather fancy it is your car coming," said Gay. "At least, it's one with very bright
headlights."

She paused as the great golden lights
drenched them in a fierce glare and then dipped.

"Yes, it's stopping."

"Confound it," muttered Sir Peter as the long
car slid in to the kerb.

The door swung open as the chauffeur hurriedly got out.

"I'm extremely sorry, Sir."

The chauffeur was breathless.

"Where the deuce have you been?"

"I misunderstood your directions, Sir."

"And where can I drop you, Miss Hamilton?" Sir Peter enquired.

As Gay looked up, she could have sworn that
the eyes under the dragged-down brim were taking in every inch of her.

"Oh, I'll walk."

"You will not. Get in, Bennett."

"Very good, Sir."

"Drive down as far as the post-office and wait
for me there."

"Right, Sir."

Bennett swung open the concave door again
and got in. Almost noiselessly, the car slid away
from the kerb, lighting up the narrow street as
it went.

"And now I have something to say to you,"

41

said Sir Peter, as they walked on. "I don't know who you are from Adam, but I'm quite sober, I can promise you that."

His manner suddenly became earnest as he went on:

"I want someone to read to me, and you have the sort of voice that I like. I will give you three hundred pounds a year if you will come and live in my house and read to me when I need you."

Gay could hardly believe her ears as he continued more slowly:

"I have a housekeeper, so the conventions will be satisfied. Three hundred a year may sound a good deal of money to you, but I may want to be read to at strange times.

"I do not sleep well, so you may be called upon to get up and read to me in the middle of the night. As a matter of fact, I have not been quite truthful," admitted Sir Peter.

He halted on the path and grinned boyishly at Gay.

"I asked Mrs. Clements who the young lady with the beautiful voice was, and she told me that it belonged to a Miss Hamilton, who was companion-help to a Miss Fortescue."

"Am I awake or dreaming?"

"Awake."

"I can't be," Gay said in a dazed voice.

"And why not?"

"Well, it's too amazing," said Gay. "And how can I decide? You may not mean it...I mean to say...tomorrow you may feel..."

"You mean you think that tomorrow I may be sober?"

"Well . . ." Gay was stammering and confused.

"Believe me, Miss Hamilton, I am sober now," Sir Peter assured her. "How long I shall be is another thing, but the fact remains that I am sober now. Where are we, by the way?"

"I can see the rear lights of the car," replied Gay. "About twenty yards away from us, I should say."

"Then let us wait a minute."

The headlights of a passing car swung past them at that moment, and Gay caught sight of the handsome face spoilt by the bitter, twisted mouth.

Suddenly she felt that this was all too queer to be true!

This man, and the darkness, and now this extraordinary proposition of his.

Three hundred a year to read to him! He didn't mean it, of course.

"Well, have you made up your mind?"

"Must I decide now?"

"No; think it over if you like."

"Do you really mean it?" asked Gay desperately. "You see, if I give up the job I have now, I really have nowhere to go. I could go home, of course, but I don't want to."

"I really mean it."

"And do you want me at once?"

"If you can come at once, yes."

"I should have to give Miss Fortescue notice."

"And forego your wages, of course."

"Yes, I suppose so," said Gay helplessly.

This was too strange to be real, she thought. And what on earth was the time? She had to be in by half-past seven.

"I wonder what the time is," she said abruptly.

"Quarter-to-eight," Sir Peter told her after a pause of a second or two. "That I can tell you more easily than you can tell me, as I have a specially made watch."

"Good Heavens, and I had to be in by half-past seven! I must go," said Gay desperately.

"And you are coming to me at Simon's Close?"

"Yes, I think I am! At least, I am sure I am if you really want me."

She gave a soft, bewildered little laugh.

"But it's rather difficult for me to alter the whole of my life all in a minute! I . . . haven't anyone to ask, and I shouldn't ask them even if I had."

"How near are you to your destination now?" enquired Sir Peter.

"Quite near."

"And we to the car?"

He had taken her arm again and was walking on.

"Almost up to it," answered Gay.

"And are you sure I cannot drop you anywhere?"

"Quite sure."

"Then good-bye," said Sir Peter gravely, baring his head. "I will expect you tomorrow afternoon and will send the car for you at half-past three. What did you say the name of your employer was?"

"Miss Fortescue," replied Gay breathlessly.

She stood as if in a dream as they came to a standstill next to the car, with Bennett standing by the side of it.

A dream! A strange, impossible dream, she thought, as she watched the tail-lamps getting smaller and smaller and at last disappearing altogether.

Only about an hour, no, much less than that, and the whole of her life had altered.

Tomorrow! She was going to live in that man's house tomorrow. Knowing nothing whatever about him.

Of course she couldn't go really. It was too preposterous, too extraordinary. Gay took two or three long, trembling breaths.

And then, as she started to walk again, the Church clock began to chime the hour.

Gay broke into a little run. Half-an-hour late! Well, perhaps it would make it easier for her to leave, because Miss Fortescue would certainly be furious.

*　　*　　*

Miss Fortescue was furious.

Opening the mean little front door, she stood in the lighted aperture, glaring.

"Where have you been?"

"To Brighton."

"The omnibus from Brighton gets to the halt at seven o'clock," said Miss Fortescue icily. "I allowed you half-an-hour from there, although it does not take half-an-hour."

Her eyes narrowed as she went on:

"Therefore, for another half-hour you have been meandering about the streets. Explain yourself."

"I am sorry I am late," mumbled Gay. "I agree that it was wrong of me, but it was inevitable."

"How do you mean 'inevitable'?" questioned Miss Fortescue sharply.

"I mean inevitable, just that," replied Gay.

She began to pull off her soft hat as she stood there, pushing her hair into place.

Her face was flushed and her eyes were bright with suppressed excitement.

"Your impertinence overwhelms me," said Miss Fortescue. "Go upstairs and change your dress and get my supper ready."

Her tone was frigid.

"And mind you, I shall not overlook this breach of discipline. I have ways of making those who work for me behave, Miss Hamilton! You will fetch in extra coal after supper."

"I shall do nothing of the kind," retorted Gay, her anger suddenly flaring.

After all, what right had this ugly little woman to speak to her as she was doing?

"Don't ... speak ... to me like that," Gay went on, and she stammered a little in her rage.

For here she was shut up in the house with this grim little woman, and there was something about her beady eyes that frightened her.

And her fear made her speak more wildly than she would have done otherwise.

She had always been afraid of Miss Fortescue and now there was something malignant about her fixed gaze.

Supposing she murdered her in the night? Supposing she...smothered her? Or drugged her? Gay's vivid imagination flamed.

The day had been an exciting one and she was overtired. It had all been too exciting, too dreadfully exciting.

Miss Fortescue stood so still...like a cat before it springs on its prey.

"Miss Hamilton! Go up to your room and remain there."

"I shall...do...nothing of the kind."

"You will do what I tell you," exclaimed Miss Fortescue, and her china teeth suddenly shone very brightly in the pale greenish gleam of the incandescent light.

"I shall...not."

"You will!" cried Miss Fortescue, and she came along the narrow hall towards Gay.

Swelling...she was swelling out like a balloon, thought Gay, sick with fear and hysterical fatigue.

Turning, she wrenched open the front door and flung herself down the narrow stone steps, and down the path and out into the road.

It was dark, with a sort of clammy dampness that struck into one's very bones. But in the house that she had just left was a horror that was worse than any amount of clamminess.

There was something baleful about Miss Fortescue, thought Gay, gasping for breath, for she had run a long way now.

47

The iron gate that she had wrenched open and banged behind her must be quite a quarter of a mile away.

She came to a trembling standstill and fumbled for her handkerchief to wipe her face. And as she stood there she suddenly realised what she had done.

Everything that she possessed, almost, was in the house next to Wally's Farm. Her hat and her nightdress and her writing materials.

Only her bag was clutched under her arm: her bag that mercifully contained her purse.

And then slowly Gay came to her senses. She was leaving Miss Fortescue anyhow, in less than twenty-four hours.

Then why hadn't she stayed there as a sane person would have done? What was she going to do in this village where she hardly knew anyone? Even for one night what could she do?

Half-past eight; the Church clock had just struck the half-hour. Gloomily, the rather discordant chimes wavered over the dark, silent village street.

Drawing a long, trembling breath, Gay suddenly remembered Mrs. Walters!

She lived behind the Church in a funny little cottage below the level of the road. No doubt it would be a bit cramped, but Gay felt certain that Norah Walters would take her in.

Oh, how wet, how frightfully wet she was! And no nightdress or toothbrush, but what did it matter? She was away from that dreadful Miss Fortescue!

Chapter Three

In the great house surrounded by trees, Mr. Fenton was doing his accounts.

His room, which had once been the library, was luxurious.

A large fire was burning in the old iron grate and the leaping flames of it were reflected in the huge oil paintings which hung on the panelled walls.

Large, decorative ancestors, in peruke wigs, with slender, dandified fingers that seemed to emerge contemptuously from the lace ruffles.

Ancestors who seemed to glance down with disdain at the mean little man who sat stooping over a massive writing-table, a cigarette between his lips.

Mr. Fenton was hurriedly writing long lists of figures, at which he was scowling.

Something would have to be done; his luck lately had been phenomenally bad!

Amalgamated Goldfields had been so wonderfully boosted in the Press, and yet when the last shaft had been sunk they had come on a spring.

And now the shares that he had bought at ninety-five were down to just below thirty-seven.

Of course there was always a chance of picking up on Associated Electricals.

Where was the evening paper? Not brought in yet; curse that fellow George.

Mr. Fenton got up from the writing-table and went over to the fire. He dragged down the handle of the old-fashioned bell and stood there waiting.

Hardly up to the high mantelshelf he reached, for Mr. Fenton was small, and somehow utterly out-of-place in the dignified setting.

"Yes, Sir."

George stood in the high opening of the old oak door.

"Where's the paper?"

"I don't know, Sir."

"Go and find out."

Mr. Fenton straddled a little in front of the fire. It was pleasant to have a brace of servants to run at your behest, he thought complacently. Servants who knew which side their bread was buttered on.

Nothing like having one's hand on the pursestrings to keep people in their places, thought Mr. Fenton, his eyes on the door.

It was always a good thing to get hold of a man who had a black mark on his record somewhere.

George and Fanny, both known to the police! That kept them quiet when their pay wasn't quite what they thought it was going to be, he thought with a smirk of satisfaction.

"Here is the paper, Sir."

"It's been unfolded! Who's had it?"

"Mrs. James, Sir."

"Ha!"

Unfolding the paper, Mr. Fenton lowered his face into it.

Just like her, defying him when she dared, and when she dared not, cringing. However, in that dotty kid of theirs he had a powerful weapon.

"All right, my girl, then my course is quite clear! It's Rockwood for that wretched kid of yours! No more private homes and what-not!"

Then she changed her tune, all right.

Mr. Fenton was grinning down into the *Evening News*. Associated Electricals had taken an upwards turn. More than Amalgamated Goldfields had, curse them!

Too late to get on to his Broker now. First thing tomorrow morning, though.

He crossed the room again. He'd taught the servants to build him up a decent fire here. Cold as a tomb it was, unless one stacked on the coal.

He sat down at his desk. There was time before dinner to go through the figures again.

Sir Peter was safe upstairs in his own rooms. Before he got some more cheques out of him, he'd see that he was well primed up. Some of the Cointreau; that would be the ticket, at about half-past nine, well after dinner.

Fanny cooked well, which was a good thing.

Nothing to complain about with the food, except the bills.

Mr. Fenton bent his horrid face to his writing-pad again, then lifted it again. Someone about in the hall; that was unusual at this time in the evening.

Someone scratching the wall with uncertain fingers; not scratching, running undecided hands over it. Feeling their way . . .

In a flash, Mr. Fenton had his writing-pad in one of the smoothly running drawers of the massive writing-table.

Sir Peter couldn't see, of course, but he could be sharp enough at times. And he looked as if he could see, that was the worst of it.

"Oh, you're here, Fenton."

The door had opened and shut again.

How did he know who was here? wondered Mr. Fenton, getting up out of his chair in a hurry.

That was the worst of him when he wasn't tight. Went on like a man who could see.

"Yes, Sir Peter."

"You've got a good fire here. It's more than I have."

Sir Peter was feeling his way across the room.

First one hand and then the other, until he reached the heavy sheepskin rug, golden and curly and splashed with firelight.

And, having reached it, he stood there, holding out his hands to the blaze that he could not see.

Long, thin hands; the heavy gold signet ring,

with the crown on it, slipping on the little finger of the left hand.

"Yes, you've got a better fire than I have, Fenton."

"I will see that yours is made up, Sir Peter."

"Where's the bell? I'll ring for someone."

Stooping a little, Sir Peter was feeling round the corner of the mantelpiece.

Mr. Fenton watched him like a cat watching a mouse. What was the matter with him tonight?

He never moved out of his own wing at this time of night, and he never gave an order either.

"Yes, Sir?"

Now it was George who had the shock of his life.

His master, downstairs at this time of the evening when he was generally tight as a lord in his own wing!

George's eyes flew to Mr. Fenton, who answered their appeal with a little upwards jerk of his chin.

"George, my fire wants attending to. It is usual for the master of the house to have as good a fire as his valet-secretary."

Sir Peter's voice was cold and deliberate.

"Yes, Sir."

"Go and put it right at once."

"Yes, Sir."

"Has he gone, Fenton?"

And now there was something a little faltering in the proud voice.

"Yes, Sir Peter."

"He's a nice boy, that. I think we ought to raise his wages, Fenton. Remind me tomorrow when we go through the accounts."

"Yes, Sir Peter."

"And now, Fenton, I have a piece of news for you," continued Sir Peter. "I have taken on someone to read to me."

He rested his arm on the mantelpiece as he went on:

"A Miss Hamilton, to whom I was introduced by Mrs. Clements this afternoon. And I could tell by her voice that she was the very person for me."

He smiled reminiscently.

"A beautiful voice, like gold. The Girl with the Golden Voice. Let's drink to it, Fenton," ended Sir Peter solemnly.

He turned his brilliant, sightless gaze to his Secretary.

"Very good, Sir."

Mr. Fenton scurried across the room to a tall mahogany cupboard with inlaid doors.

And as he hurried his mind was busy. Taken on someone to read to him! For how long every day was she coming to Simon's Close? And who was she?

"Whisky or brandy, Sir Peter?"

"Brandy."

"A spot of soda with it, Sir?"

"Certainly not," returned Sir Peter.

He stood there, swaying very slightly on his feet. He looked shabby, and his waistcoat wanted cleaning, for it was spotted with food-stains.

'He looks as if he could see me through and

through,' thought Mr. Fenton as he crossed the room with two brimming glasses in his hands.

"Here's to her health, Fenton. The Girl with the Golden Voice!"

Without even a pause, Sir Peter tossed off the brandy. And as it ran glowing through his veins he smiled.

"I think she must be beautiful, Fenton," he remarked. "Young and beautiful. And she's coming here to live. We must speak to Mrs. James. We'll put her near me, as she will read to me if I can't sleep."

"Coming here to live?"

Mr. Fenton was taken off his guard.

He stood there staring at his employer. Coming there to live! Going to read to his employer when he couldn't sleep.

Getting her nose into the house and worming her way into the favour of the master of it.

Who was she? Who was this young woman when she was at home? wondered Mr. Fenton, forgetting the brandy glowing sympathetically in the cut-glass tumbler.

"You were outside in the car when we were in the post-office," said Sir Peter expansively.

"Don't tell me that you didn't see her, Fenton. What was she like? Young, slim? Fair as the lily or dark as the rose?"

Then Mr. Fenton's mind gave an uncomfortable leap.

The girl he had followed across the fields! Just like his luck! Coming into the house all ready to do him down. Not she; he'd get even with her first.

Mr. Fenton thought quickly.

"Yes, I think I saw her, Sir."

"Think you saw her. Where were your eyes, man?"

"Well, she wasn't the type that one takes much stock of, Sir."

Mr. Fenton spoke slowly and deliberately.

"Although I didn't hear her voice, of course. But if it's the young lady I mean, she's not very much to look at! Rather the masculine type, and I never have cared for that."

His tone was malignant as he went on:

"Suspicion of a moustache, and not much of a complexion. She came out of the post-office just before you and the Vicar and his lady."

"Yes, that must be Miss Hamilton."

As Sir Peter stood there, his sensation of disappointment almost overwhelmed him. And he could have sworn . . .

He had *felt* that he had seen her: slender and delicate, with a face like an upturned flower with its little white chin like a petal.

And now! Living in his house! Reading to him at night! With her weather-beaten face and moustache thrown in.

What a fool he had made of himself!

But Fenton must never know it. No, he would have her there as he had promised her, and she was relying on it, and then he would get rid of her.

One could get rid of anyone if it was made sufficiently worth their while.

Miss Mannering, for instance. She must have been pleased with all that money, poor thing.

"How did Miss Mannering like her month's extra pay, Fenton?"

And now Sir Peter's sightless gaze was on his Secretary again.

"She was delighted, Sir."

"Splendid. I always felt sorry for that woman," said Sir Peter slowly, "although her voice got on my nerves."

"Yes, Sir. But you will not have that to contend with in Miss Hamilton."

Mr. Fenton's tone was smooth.

"And I always say that handsome is as handsome does, and if the young lady has a good reading voice, we can't complain that she's not the successful entrant for a beauty competition, can we, Sir?"

"No."

"And as to her sleeping-accommodation, Sir, I'll see Mrs. James about it. Where would you like her put, Sir?"

"I told you: near my room."

"Very good, Sir."

"She is to have a salary of three hundred a year, Fenton."

"Three hundred a year, Sir?"

"Yes. I think I was more than a little tight when I mentioned that figure, but, having mentioned it, the figure must stand, Fenton."

"It's enormous, Sir."

"It is. More than you get yourself."

"Yes, Sir."

"But I daresay you make it up in other ways, Fenton."

"I beg your pardon, Sir?"

Now Mr. Fenton was on his dignity. That always went down with this blind man, he had found.

A poor thing a blind man was, thought Mr. Fenton contemptuously. Always on the alert to think he was a bother.

Dependent, that's what blindness made you —dependent. Blindness and drink; they went well together so far as he, Arthur Fenton, was concerned.

Mr. Fenton came nearer to the tall, motionless figure holding out thin hands to the blaze.

"We must see about another waistcoat for you, Sir," he pointed out blandly. "This one's spotted something shocking. We mustn't let the young lady see you like this, Sir Peter."

"Spotted? What with?"

The aesthetic-looking face was stained with a heavy flush. Food, of course, although Fenton was too decent to say so!

What it was to be blind! The undying humiliation of it! How long had he to endure this sort of thing?

And then the thought that never really left him when he was sober fled across his mind again.

To end it all! How could he do it?

To end these eternal days and endless nights and the ghastly waking to another eternal day. He would do it one day, but how?

"I'll get out another suit tomorrow morning, Sir," continued Mr. Fenton. "What time is the young lady coming, Sir?"

"I shall send the car down at about three. She's at a small house next to Wally's Farm. And now, Fenton, what about another glass of brandy? I'm sorry I said that about your making it up in other ways.

"I didn't mean it, as you know. I don't know what I should do without you, Fenton."

Mr. Fenton's eyes narrowed as he hurried over to the corner cupboard again, an empty tumbler in each hand.

He would have to do something about that three hundred pounds a year: that couldn't be allowed for one moment, of course.

And thinking about it, Mr. Fenton took quite a long time to fill up the tumblers again.

*   *   *

Gay slept dreamlessly. The feather bed at Norah Walters' house was sublimely comfortable, and her bed at Miss Fortescue's had not been comfortable.

Also, at Miss Fortescue's there had always been a background of something hateful, something that lay couched behind her dreams and was there waiting for her when she awoke.

So, in the small bed-room with the sloping roof, she slept until Norah stood at her elbow with a tray.

"Norah, whatever time is it?"

Gay lay there and blinked.

"Half-past nine, Miss Gay," replied Norah.

She put the tray down on the little white-painted table beside the bed.

"I've got your trunk downstairs."

"My trunk! Norah, how did you get it? Do tell me!"

Gay's eyes were bright with excitement.

"I went round before seven. I always keep a key, as you know," said Norah.

"I got the old girl's tea, and I told her that she ought to be ashamed of herself and that you were going to have the police on her if she didn't send along with me your things and the money due to you."

She grinned with satisfaction.

"I said I'd taken you in and that it was a toss-up if you didn't get pneumonia, and that if you did she'd be had up for manslaughter."

"Norah!"

"I did, and she was in no end of a state. Told me to go and pack your things at once, and said that she owed you three weeks' wages and I could take it to you. And here it is!"

Norah beamed from ear to ear.

"Take it all, Norah," Gay pleaded with an affectionate smile.

"Take it all? Never." Norah shook her head emphatically. "You'll need it before you're done, Miss Gay. I'll take just ten shillings, and that'll help me more than you can ever know.

"I'll give Jim a shilling of it because he brought his barrow round for your trunk."

"Oh, Norah, take more!"

"No, thank you, Miss Gay. It's been a pleasure to me to have you under my roof, and I'll gladly keep you here for as long as you'd like to stay."

She patted Gay's arm affectionately.

"And now you eat your breakfast while I open your trunk for you."

"Norah, I must brush my teeth."

Gay kicked back the bed-clothes and stood on the rag mat, slim in the old-fashioned night-dress. Her eyes shone and her lips were scarlet in her pale face.

"Pretty as a picture," Norah told her husband a minute later as she held the kettle over a big white jug.

"She oughtn't to go to Simon's Close, and I don't know what to do about it."

"You can't do anything, my girl," countered Jim cheerfully. "But tell the young lady that she's welcome here if anything goes wrong at the Close. Now I'm off. Where's that shilling you promised me?"

* * *

It was half-past three much sooner than Gay thought it would be.

Time goes fast when one is apprehensive, and Gay had suddenly become apprehensive.

The car was to meet her outside the post-office, Norah had settled all that, and her trunk had gone up to Simon's Close with a message to that effect.

"Who shall we send the message to?" enquired Gay when Norah proposed this scheme.

"Mrs. James."

"Who is Mrs. James, Norah, and how do you know about her?"

"Everyone knows about Simon's Close, Miss

Gay, and Mrs. James is the housekeeper," replied Norah.

It was not necessary to tell this girl that Mrs. James was either Mr. Fenton's mistress or his wife. Nobody quite knew which, and Sir Peter himself had no idea that she might be either.

There was a child, so the village declared: an idiot child who was put away, but put away somewhere very comfortably.

Rumour ran high about Simon's Close. The whole thing was a scandal, so the village maintained, and that Fenton ought to be jailed.

But it was useless to say a word to Sir Peter, because he thought the world of him.

Keeps him plied with drink and that's what's got him his cushy job and keeps it for him, too, said the village, and the village knew what it was talking about.

And now Gay stood gazing at Norah.

"Of course; Sir Peter told me that there was a housekeeper," she said. "I'd forgotten that. It's all happened so suddenly that I've forgotten most things."

Now, as Gay stood by the door of the post-office, her heart beating in her throat, she thought how lovely and happy a thing it was to have had an insight into a home such as she had just left.

For Norah and her husband were happy together, although they were dreadfully poor.

That was love, thought Gay, her eyes soft and tender. Two people all in all to each other and able to show it in loving, practical ways.

Norah's face was loving as she set the meal

before Jim, a Jim who had just washed his hands and face at the sink. The way he looked at her and thanked her made Gay feel very warm.

It would be heavenly to be able to cook for someone you loved and see him eating with a good appetite.

Those were the real things, thought Gay, who was feeling tremulous and upset now that she had left the little house where everything was peace and harmony.

What was she going into now?

To begin with, how was she going to face that hateful man who had followed her through the field? She would be under the same roof with him.

What was the new life going to be like?

The car would soon be here; it was five-and-twenty past three. That huge car and the grand chauffeur.

Or perhaps it wouldn't come at all. Perhaps Sir Peter hadn't meant it! He had been intoxicated at the time he had made the suggestion of her going there; he had said so quite frankly.

Then, supposing the whole thing was just nothing and she had no job at all? What was she going to do?

Where, for instance, would she go, say at a quarter-to-four? Back to Norah, of course. But she couldn't stay with Norah indefinitely.

Gay turned and stared into the window of the post-office. If that car didn't come she would die! She wouldn't be able to go on at all. It *had* to come!

She would look such a fool—such a hopeless fool. She had told people she was going there. She had even written to her mother.

The next collection was at three-thirty. If the postman came before the car, she would know that it wasn't coming, because sometimes postmen who collected were a minute or two late. And a chauffeur like Bennett would never be late. . . .

And then came the great, hoarse bark of a powerful motor horn. Probably some touring-car rushing through the village, thought Gay, continuing to stare in through the post-office window, because the people inside couldn't see her.

It was all notepaper and books and notices about whist drives, and the box for the letters: that took up quite a lot of room.

And Bennett had to open the door and get out onto the path before she turned.

And it was not at all what he had intended to do, for Bennett knew which side his bread was buttered on, and which side Fenton had made quite clear.

"If that wretched girl is coming here, she's jolly well got to toe the line," he had snarled, and his ugly mouth had looked uglier than usual.

"None of your 'Miss' this and 'Miss' that, Bennett my boy. Let her get into the car herself, and don't you lift her suitcase for her either."

But Gay's frightened start as she turned quite disarmed Bennett, who was really quite a decent young man and had a girl of his own at Brighton.

"For Simon's Close, Miss?" he asked politely.

"Y-yes," stammered Gay.

"I'll take your case, Miss."

He opened the door behind the driver's seat. And then, getting back into his place, he slammed the door and carefully let in the clutch.

The huge car slid noiselessly away from the kerb, its long, pale bonnet pointing rather disdainfully down the village street.

Chapter Four

The morning at Simon's Close had been stormy, for at dawn Mr. Fenton had broken to Mrs. James that a young lady called Miss Hamilton was coming to take Miss Mannering's place.

"But she's going to live in," Mr. Fenton told her, "and she's as pretty as a peach."

"How long have you known?"

"Never you mind," said Mr. Fenton tantalisingly.

He turned over again and went back to sleep, while Mrs. James lay shivering as the light began to come slowly up behind the pinewoods.

"Pretty as a peach!"

She knew what that would mean. Hell and torture for her. For, oddly enough, she really loved the hateful man who had ruined her life.

Their child... Mrs. James thought about him as she dressed. So loving and so simple in his ways. People said that his little brain was clouded, but that was because they didn't know.

As Mrs. James combed her hair she began to think about the last time she had seen him. She had taken him a woolly bear and he had smiled so prettily and held out his arms for it.

The matron had said that he was beginning to take notice. Beginning to take notice! Why, for years he had known every word she said, the pretty dear.

But it was better for him to be where he was, because she had to earn a living and so had Arthur.

And Arthur had been so good in letting Basil stay where he was. Although he sometimes held it over her that if she ... And then Mrs. James trembled a little as she stuck in a hair-pin.

But he had promised to marry her when he could. He had a wife already, but she had known that all along. But she would die sometime, thought Mrs. James, settling herself into her neat black dress.

And then with what they had saved they would start a little business and have Basil to live with them.

Mrs. James finished her dressing and went out to the kitchen.

Fanny was a late riser, but she was an uncommonly good cook, and the girl, Elsie, would have put on the kettle.

They really ought to have more servants for such a big house, but Arthur said that they couldn't. And Arthur knew, thought Mrs. James, opening the kitchen door.

Then she closed it quickly behind her. Arthur didn't like to be disturbed until she took him his early tea. And he would be disturbed if the door was left open.

Fanny was in one of her rages: she had been out the night before and had probably had something to drink.

She stood at the table, holding on to one white corner of it. Yes, she had undoubtedly had something to drink, and not the night before, either.

"Where's that Fenton?"

Fanny was yelling out loudly.

"Fanny, be quiet; Mr. Fenton might hear you."

Mrs. James came quietly across the stone-flagged floor. She was not afraid of the red-faced woman who stood there shouting. Mrs. James was not afraid of anyone, except the man she loved.

But Fanny was past taking any notice of anyone.

"He's cut my salary!" she shouted.

She waved a slip of paper in her hand.

"Fifty-two pounds a year I get here, and I'm going to have it, too. Four pounds a month isn't fifty-two pounds a year. Go and fetch him or I will!"

Fanny made a rush for the door.

"Elsie, is the kettle on?" asked Mrs. James.

With trembling hands she took a cup down from the dresser.

"Kettle! I'll kettle him!" cried Fanny furiously.

And then began a struggle for possession of the door-handle.

George, sauntering in, buttoning up his coat,

stopped short at the sight of the scrimmage at the door, and then bolted across the floor to join in.

"She's tight," he said, gasping. "Been singing and carrying on proper all night. I heard her."

"I'm no more tight than you are, you dirty jail-bird," yelled Fanny.

She gave up the door-handle to fly at George, while Elsie devoted herself to the kettle and tried not to hear or see what was going on.

For it was an awful place to be in, thought Elsie tearfully, and if she had a proper home of her own to go to she never would stay.

But you had to stay where you were put for at least a year, reflected Elsie sadly, if you'd been to an approved school.

Then the kitchen door opened.

"Now then, what's all this?"

Mr. Fenton was wearing Sir Peter's cast-off dressing-gown, which was made of thick silk and was still in excellent condition.

The only thing was that it was much too long for him, and the deep hem that Mrs. James had turned up made it look rather odd.

"You—!"

Fanny let loose a stream of abuse.

"Number four-three-seven giving trouble again," said Mr. Fenton smoothly.

And he laughed out loud as Fanny shrank and paled.

"Get on with your work, you little fool," he snapped, "or you know what you'll get. You've been drinking, of course. Where did you get it from?"

Mr. Fenton came forward menacingly.

"I bought it."

"The police'd believe that, wouldn't they?" sneered Mr. Fenton. "Get on with your work, I tell you."

He turned sharply on the others.

"And you, George, and you, Elsie. A collection of jail-birds I've got to work for me. God, I don't know why I do it. I'll report every one of you to Sir Peter and see that he gives you the sack."

He looked round at them and sneered.

"I'll get Sergeant Ward up here and tell him about your thieving ways. A proper convict-crew, and that's the gospel truth."

Mr. Fenton railed on Mrs. James.

"Where's my tea?"

"It's just ready, Arthur."

"Just ready! It ought to have been ready half-an-hour ago. I'll go back to my room and you bring it along to me. And if I hear another sound..."

Mr. Fenton stared round the silent kitchen.

Fanny, breathing rather heavily, was walking slowly towards the big range.

Elsie, with her mouth open, was shaking with terror.

George was stooping to a cupboard and taking out a boot-brush.

In the low-ceilinged kitchen, only a collection of cringing, beaten human beings, thought Mrs. James, knowing herself to be one of them.

And yet, what else could she do? Basil... it was all for Basil, her little son, her darling.

70

But the morning that had begun so badly went on from bad to worse.

A room had to be prepared for Miss Hamilton.

"As far away from mine as possible," ordered Sir Peter when he was consulted.

For he too had suffered a violent revulsion of feeling.

He had saddled himself with an ugly girl for a month; for of course she would not stay longer than that.

But a month was only fair, as she had given up another post to come to him.

"You said last night that you wished her in your wing," Mr. Fenton pointed out smoothly.

"Did I? Then I have changed my mind," said Sir Peter curtly. "Put her near Mrs. James, on the corridor above me."

"Very good, Sir Peter."

Mr. Fenton grinned to himself and went away to find Mrs. James.

"Miss Hamilton is to have the bed-room next to yours," he told her with a cruel smile.

Mrs. James flushed scarlet.

"I won't have it!" she cried passionately. "I've borne enough from you without that last insult."

"Be careful now, Annie."

"I don't care," flamed Mrs. James. "I'm sick to death of it and I won't have it. I'd rather leave the house."

"All right, all right," said Mr. Fenton. "I was only pulling your leg! Sir Peter doesn't know where you sleep, does he? He said, 'Put her next to Mrs. James on the corridor above me.'"

He smirked.

"Well, that's where he thinks you are, and there's no need for him to think anything else, is there, old girl?"

"Arthur . . ."

"Get along with you, and get her room ready! And no fal-lals or luxuries in it, either!

"She's got to toe the line, and the sooner she knows it the better. And no early tea being carried up there, mind. Understand me?"

His voice was bitter as he went on:

"We don't want her here, and the sooner we can get rid of her, the better for all of us. See?"

"Yes," said Mrs. James thankfully, and she hurried off along the corridors.

Endless corridors with endless rooms leading off them. Empty, uncared-for rooms, and icy cold.

Round the corners scurried Mrs. James, suddenly drawing herself up with a little scream as she almost ran into her employer.

"I'm so sorry I frightened you. Is it Mrs. James?" queried Sir Peter kindly.

Mrs. James, gazing up at him, thought to herself that it was a dreadful thing that any man should look so uncared for.

His waistcoat . . . it was really a disgrace. She would love to sponge it herself, but she dared not suggest it to Arthur.

And his hair . . . the parting was all that was wrong there, anyhow. His shaving he seemed able to manage, and his hands were always well kept.

But the whole look of him was tragic, thought Mrs. James, suddenly overwhelmed by it.

For she so rarely saw him face to face; only Mr. Fenton went in and out of his rooms, and George took up his meals.

The old banqueting-hall had not been used for months, for years. The old paintings were shrouded in dust sheets, and the chairs too were covered over.

Simon's Close was like an old baronial Castle that marauders had left destitute. Two or three rooms were habitable, and all the rest had been given up to the voiceless spirits that frequent deserted rooms.

"Are you getting a room on the south corridor ready for Miss Hamilton?"

"Yes, Sir."

"Make it bright for her, as she is only a young girl."

"Yes, Sir."

"And I look to you to see that she has all she wants, Mrs. James. I know Mr. Fenton will do all he can, but a woman can do more for another woman than a man can."

"Yes, Sir Peter."

"Where will she have her meals, Mrs. James?"

"Where would you wish, Sir?"

"For her to have them in her own sitting-room would entail too much work, perhaps?"

So she was to have a sitting-room as well! Arthur had said nothing about that.

"It would mean a good deal of extra carrying up trays, Sir."

"But why should that matter? Money is no object, at least not to that extent. Take on an extra servant."

He thought for a moment.

"Get in touch with Mrs. Clements. She probably knows of a village girl who would be glad to come. Offer her a pound a week; that would be a fair wage as the wages of this household go."

"Very good, Sir."

Mrs. James stood there watching Sir Peter feel his way along the cold wall.

Another servant at a wage of a pound a week! Arthur would raise hell!

A village girl in the house, carrying tales about what went on in the kitchen and elsewhere. Out of the question. What was to be done about it?

Mrs. James went down the shallow staircase at a run.

But Mr. Fenton was equal to the occasion.

"Elsie can wait on her," he said calmly. "And that young brother of George's can come in and help Fanny—he's just left school."

He snorted.

"Sitting-room indeed! Well, I suppose she'll have to have it. But it won't be for long, I'll see to that!

"Elsie!"

"Yes, Sir?"

"You're to wait on the young lady that's coming," ordered Mr. Fenton. "And if I find you carrying tales to her about what goes on down here, I'll flay you alive, and don't you forget it."

"Yes, Sir," whispered Elsie, her dark, furtive eyes alight with terror.

*   *   *

Gay never forgot her first sight of Simon's Close.

There it stood, shrouded with trees, the long grey front of it and the two side-wings.

"It is frowning at me," said Gay to herself as she stared along the avenue. "Not only frowning, but scowling."

And the appalling neglect of it! The hedges wanted clipping, beautiful high yew hedges that must have been hundreds of years old.

The paths than ran off the main avenue were covered with weeds.

And now they were sweeping round a curve that brought the house into full view. A beautiful house, if only it had been taken care of. Tall, mullioned windows, most of them without curtains.

And a small front door, looking like a little old man whose burden is too heavy for him to bear, lost among the high windows and turreted roof.

The car swept round a piece of lawn dotted over with flower-beds, among which a man was working.

He straightened himself at the sound of the soft hiss of tyres on gravel, stared at the car and its occupants, then bent over his spade again.

"I'll ring the bell, Miss."

Bennett, who had got out of the car, was wondering who would open the door.

Fenton, more likely than not, he thought to himself, wanting to get in first with this pretty young thing with her innocent face.

Odd, the whole thing was odd, thought

Bennett, giving the bell a second good tug as there had been no response to the first.

Then the front door opened and Mrs. James stood there. And from the car Gay saw the look in her eyes, and she shivered. Heavens! Was anyone ever so unwelcome as she obviously was?

What on earth had she come for?

She got out of the car and stood there, oddly dignified with her upright carriage.

"Mrs. James?" she enquired.

Gay squeezed her suede bag a little closer to her side to give her confidence.

"Yes."

Mrs. James stood a little aside to allow Gay to come into the hall.

And as she stood aside her whole soul rose up in hatred at the sight of the young girl. A trick of Arthur's, of course, to get this beautiful young thing under his roof.

'She should not stay here,' thought Mrs. James, trembling inside her neat black dress.

"I will show you your rooms," she said stiffly, "and have your trunk sent upstairs. This way."

Mrs. James turned and led Gay along the stone-flagged hall, freezing cold in the chill November afternoon, and then up the great branched stairway to the first corridor.

Gay never forgot that first sensation of deadly cold. Even the high walls looked cold, with their huge oil paintings dividing them up into coloured oblongs.

And now up more stairs and along another corridor. Here the doors were smaller and shaped like Church doors.

Turning the iron-ringed handle of one of them, Mrs. James opened it.

"This is your sitting-room," she announced, "and this is your bed-room opening out of it."

"Oh yes."

Gay tried to speak pleasantly, but her lips felt numb. There was no fire. And it all looked so ghastly. The bed-room . . . all so shabby!

On the bed was one of those thick cotton quilts such as servants used to have in their bed-rooms.

The dressing-table was huge and massive, and without any mats to make it look less dreadful.

And only one candle in an ugly china candlestick. Was there, then, no electric light? Yes, there were wires hanging from the ceiling, and even wall brackets, but there were no globes inside them.

Well, she had only just arrived. She would wait and see before she said anything.

"You will have a young girl named Elsie to wait on you," said Mrs. James, "but I should like to warn you about her. She has been to an approved school and therefore you must be careful how you speak to her."

She adopted a superior tone.

"Sir Peter is very philanthropic, and so is Mr. Fenton, and between them they try to do all they can to help the unfortunate. Elsie is a good girl in her way, but she has to be kept in her place."

"What is an approved school?" asked Gay.

She stood and gazed round her. She would

never be able to stay here, of course. It was perfectly ghastly. Everything was so old!

In the middle of the room was a round table that had once been polished, and had also been beautiful at one time, but now it was faded and marked with stains.

Someone had set something hot down on it, leaving a pale ring where it had stood.

And someone else had very nearly set fire to it, by leaving an iron standing on it, thought Gay, gazing at the dark stain, her thoughts in a whirl.

It was like a horrid dream, she reflected.

The sofa, with its spindly legs and faded cushions.

The one easy-chair, which looked the reverse of anything approaching easy.

And the open, empty grate: that was worse than all the other things put together.

"An approved school is where they send young girls instead of sending them to prison," said Mrs. James, her voice breaking in on Gay's thoughts.

"I see."

Gay was wondering what would happen if she said then and there that she must go away at once!

Her trunk need not even come up the cold, chill staircase, and if it was not possible to send her in the car, she would walk back to where she had come from!

Nothing, nothing, would induce her to stay in this ghastly place.

Gay was staring at Mrs. James and wondering how she should begin to say all that she had to say. That it had all been a grave mistake . . .

"So Miss Hamilton has arrived!"

Mrs. James turned swiftly as the dapper figure of Mr. Fenton approached across the floor.

Gay wondered what she should do and say. Should she tell him she had decided that the place would not suit her? That it was too cold, too far from everywhere, and too altogether dreadful?

Mr. Fenton's voice was ingratiating as he rubbed his hands together.

"Leave us, please."

He dismissed Mrs. James with a jerk of his head.

"I have one or two matters to discuss with Miss Hamilton before she begins her duties here. And it's cold in this room. Send Elsie up to light a fire."

"Very well."

Trembling with rage, Mrs. James left the room.

Gay, for the first time since she had got into the car outside the post-office, relaxed. A fire! This man was obviously a cad, but he had suggested a fire, and for that she owed him a debt of gratitude.

She smiled pleasantly.

"It is frightfully cold."

And at that smile, and at the long dark lashes resting on the young cheek, Mr. Fenton registered a sudden vow. He would get this girl for his own at any cost!

That wretched, skinny woman who hung

round his neck like a bit of unhewn granite, and was just about as appetising, might go to hell for all he cared.

Saddling him with that idiot child, which would live forever, because they always did!

He would get rid of her; he would get rid of her somehow. One always could if one went about it the right way.

'Go at it carefully and do not rush at things,' thought Mr. Fenton, trying to keep his thoughts in check, for he had a lot of leeway to make up with this lovely thing.

Following her had been a bad break on his part, and it was not the sort of silly thing that he generally did either. But he would put that straight all right, in time.

"Yes, it's uncommonly cold up here," he observed. "We must put that right at once. And it looks cheerless, too. A young lady like you wants dainty things about her.

"I'll see what I can do about it. And I'll have tea sent up to you at once."

He paused deliberately before he went on:

"I'd like to have a word with you about Sir Peter, Miss Hamilton—that is to say, before you start work with him. He's a tragic case, really."

"Because he's blind?"

"Yes, but not only that, Miss Hamilton. I've known him for very many years, and he has this sad failing. . . ."

Mr. Fenton faltered.

"You mean . . ." Gay hesitated.

"Well, we won't put it into words," said Mr. Fenton sympathetically. "We can't blame him—"

He stopped short.

"Why? Is there anything else?" Gay asked.

Mr. Fenton tapped his forehead with two thin fingers.

"Undoubtedly! He does such strange things. You won't notice it, of course, but I, who know him so well . . ."

"Oh."

Gay felt a sudden depression descend as Mr. Fenton continued:

"I should like you to regard me as your friend, and if you are ever in any difficulty, please feel free to come to me."

He waved his arms expressively.

"All Sir Peter's affairs are in my hands. I read him his letters and write them, too. I manage the staff, pay the bills, and look after the estate. And believe me, Miss, I have my hands full."

"I am sure you have."

"And now, one more matter."

Mr. Fenton's tone was at its silkiest.

"I've come up against a good deal of unpleasantness and difficulty from time to time because there's some fellow round about this neighbourhood who might be taken for my double.

"Thank goodness I don't resemble him in some respects, if what they say is true."

He watched her closely as he continued:

"I thought I'd better tell you, Miss, because once or twice the talk has been something cruel and has brought me pretty near the police-courts, too."

"Good Heavens!"

Gay had quite forgotten that her first sight of

this man as he came into her sitting-room had definitely established his identity as that of the man who had tried to kiss her in the field.

But now she felt quite differently about him. To begin with, he had ordered her a fire, and if there was one thing that she detested more than all others it was being cold.

And then he had said that he would have her rooms made prettier, when that stiff little woman in the black dress had seemed to think that it was perfectly all right.

"Good Heavens!" she repeated.

"Ah, have you heard something, Miss?"

Mr. Fenton's furtive eyes were making a great effort to look surprised, and were succeeding.

"Oh no, not really," said Gay lamely.

She smiled again, a little timidly this time.

"I should like some tea," she said.

"And you shall have it," Mr. Fenton assured her eagerly.

He turned to leave the room.

"Here is Elsie to light your fire."

Then he ran down the corridor, and Mr. Fenton hardly ever ran. But his head was in a whirl.

"I could be a better man," he was saying to himself. "I could be a better man if only she would look at me sometimes.

"She's lovely, like some lovely spring flower coming up all by itself in the cool green grass.

"And if anyone tries to put their oar in what is going to be mine, they won't live long enough to remember what it was like the day before yesterday," he muttered as he ran.

He'd have all her rooms made to look dainty and lovely when she was sitting with Sir Peter. Every room should be stripped to fill hers, the little lovely thing.

Fanny, standing by the range, started when she saw his transformed face.

"Get Miss Hamilton's tea ready," he ordered. "And I'll take it up myself. Where's Mrs. James?"

"Here."

"Get out the glass tray with the sampler, and look sharp about it. And the best china. And the best tea."

"Why?"

"Keep your mouth shut," retorted Mr. Fenton brutally. "Now then, Fanny, get busy."

"Very good, Sir."

"And where's George? I want him."

Mr. Fenton was pacing about the kitchen.

"Those rooms you've got ready are a disgrace, Mrs. James. Not a thing in them fit to be seen. That'll have to be altered. We'll do it after tea. That kettle not boiling yet, Fanny?"

"Just on, Sir."

"I'll come back for it."

And then Mr. Fenton was gone.

Fanny winked at her husband, who had just come in and was standing there buttoning up his coat, and made a beckoning gesture with her finger.

"What's up?" asked George amiably.

"We've taken a toss for the little filly upstairs."

Fanny whispered the words as she bent over the hissing kettle.

83

"So it's for you and me to change our tune, George my boy. Everything for the young-un and nothing for the old-un, from now onwards. You get me?"

"I do," replied George laconically, and he walked briskly towards the dresser as Mr. Fenton came into the kitchen again.

* * *

After tea Gay felt very much better.

Elsie was crouched over the grate in the sitting-room, waiting until the fire burnt up properly.

That had been Mr. Fenton's order. He had come up while Gay was having her tea.

"You will excuse me?"

"Certainly."

"I am very anxious that you should feel comfortable and at home," said Mr. Fenton.

He stood by the mantelpiece, fiddling with a green glass paperweight that stood on it.

"When you are with Sir Peter a little later in the evening, I shall take the liberty to make some additions to the furniture in both these rooms."

"Thank you very much."

"The fact is," continued Mr. Fenton, casting a contemptuous glance down at Elsie's stooping back, "we have very raw material to deal with here.

"It's a constant worry to get this girl, for instance, to remember anything that she's told."

"Oh."

"Yes, I have my hands full."

He squared his shoulders importantly.

"But I would work them to the bone for Sir Peter, that fine and afflicted man. Such a tragedy." He sighed heavily.

"Can't anything be done?" asked Gay.

She sat back a little in her chair, and Mr. Fenton, seeing the eager blue eyes between the long lashes, shifted his gaze.

He felt that if he looked long at her he would go mad! And that wouldn't do at all, not yet. He must go slowly!

He must settle that skinny incubus downstairs first!

"No, and he's seen all the best men," Mr. Fenton replied. "They all say that it's hopeless. It's a paralysis of the optic-nerve; at least, I think that's what they say.

"Hand-grenade went off in front of him or something, I forget exactly how it happened, as I never speak of it, of course."

Mr. Fenton shook his head.

"But he's a strange man. Er—may I sit down, Miss?"

"Yes, do, please."

"And you get along downstairs, Elsie," said Mr. Fenton brusquely, "and mind there's plenty of coal up here for Miss Hamilton's fire. Have you showed her where the bath-room is?"

"Yes, Sir," replied Elsie, standing up and putting her dirty hands behind her back.

"Yes, she's shown me everything, thank you," interposed Gay.

She smiled a quick little smile that sent Elsie scuttling downstairs with a glowing heart.

"It's the first time anyone has smiled at me

85

since I left school," she said to George afterwards. "Not counting you, of course, you great silly, you!"

As Mr. Fenton sat in the low chair on one side of the leaping flames, Gay, looking at him, wondered how it was possible that two men in the same place could be so alike.

For she could have sworn that this was the man who had tried to kiss her. And yet of course it wasn't.

To begin with, no-one in the position in which Mr. Fenton found himself here would be such a fool. And then the way he talked . . .

But was Sir Peter what Mr. Fenton had said —lacking mentally somehow? She would find out for herself, of course. And soon.

Mr. Fenton had apparently now finished what he had to say and was getting up.

"Sir Peter told me to bring you along to his room at half-past five," he pointed out, "and it's nearly that now."

"Oh!"

Gay put a hand quickly up to her hair, which curled over her small ears and clustered round her soft neck.

"He can't see you, you know," explained Mr. Fenton suddenly.

"No, I know," said Gay, and she flushed scarlet.

"You won't forget what I told you about him? As kind a gentleman as ever walked, but very peculiar in his ways."

"I shall find all that out for myself," said Gay abruptly.

Suddenly Mr. Fenton annoyed her. He seemed to assume that she was a perfect fool and that Sir Peter was mentally deficient!

Well, the man who had come out of that inn was certainly not mentally deficient.

Drunk he was, and Gay shivered as she remembered it. But he had talked rationally enough, and he had known that he was drunk.

Feeble-minded people didn't know when they were not quite themselves, did they? Although of course it had been an astounding thing for him to take her on as his Secretary, as he had done.

Gay stood there and wondered if Mr. Fenton would go, so that she could go into her bed-room and comb her hair. Even though Sir Peter could not see her, she owed it to him.

"I'll come back for you in ten minutes," said Mr. Fenton, and then he slipped out the door like a greasy shadow.

Gay, watching him leave, wondered what it was about him that was so definitely repulsive.

He evidently wanted to be kind, and as he obviously ran everything, that was a very important thing for her.

And that little woman who had greeted her upon her arrival was positively hostile.

That was a bother, thought Gay, lighting the one candle that the bed-room possessed and watching the great gawky shadows that it projected onto the high ceiling.

But women always mistrusted other women, and not without reason, thought Gay drily.

If Mr. Fenton was going to lay himself out to

make her really comfortable, things would be made very much easier for her.

Perhaps he would put some electric bulbs in-to the shades before she came back from seeing Sir Peter, and give her a better bed-cover and maybe an eiderdown, although now that she had a fire, nothing seemed to matter, thought Gay happily.

Elsie had been told to bring her up early tea at a quarter-to-eight in the morning.

And dinner at half-past seven. That would be fun, to have meals in her sitting-room.

Rather different from those ghastly evenings with Miss Fortescue.

Miss Fortescue! Why, all that seemed like another life, thought Gay, as she brushed her hair until it shone like silk in the candlelight.

After dinner she would unpack and get everything settled, and then perhaps have a bath and go to bed early.

Gay went back into the sitting-room again. She would be glad to get the first interview with her new employer over.

That sort of thing was always rather nerve-shattering. Besides, the whole thing had been so odd.

"May I come in, Miss?"

Mr. Fenton had put on another coat and had combed his hair. He stood there staring about him.

"We'll have this looking better in another hour," he told her. "You'll be about an hour with Sir Peter, I expect, as he'll like you to read the evening paper to him."

He shrugged his shoulders.

"The lady that used to do that got the order of the boot in a hurry a couple of days ago, and he misses it."

"I see."

Now Gay felt perfectly certain in her own mind that she did not like Mr. Fenton at all. There was something crawling, something Uriah Heep-ish, about him.

"We'll get along, shall we?"

He led the way out the door and along the corridor. There was nothing but closed doors and dim lights.

Now down a flight of stone stairs; old, old stairs, thought Gay, imagining that she could feel their coldness through her shoes.

Now more closed doors, and then Mr. Fenton was tapping at one right at the end of the corridor.

"Come in."

How often in later years did that first sight of her employer in his own home come before Gay's young eyes?

Sunk in a low chair in front of a blazing fire, with his hands hanging listlessly over the high arms of it.

Alone and sightless and with *nothing to do*.

As she stood there waiting for Mr. Fenton to lead her forward, Gay registered a passionate vow.

So long as she had breath in her body, and so long as he would allow her to, she would dedicate herself to this man, she thought breathlessly.

All in one fleeting second it rushed over her like a flame!

That meeting outside the little country inn had not been a chance meeting at all. It had been foreordained, predestined!

It was her mission! As some people felt it was their mission to devote themselves to lepers.

She would take care of him, do things for him, so that life wouldn't be only a succession of hellish days and worse nights. . . .

"I have brought Miss Hamilton, Sir Peter."

Mr. Fenton was now cursing the stupidity that had caused him to tell his employer that his waistcoat was spotted with food.

For young girls were impressionable and first impressions were important. If she had seen him untidy, with a stained waistcoat, she would never have forgotten it.

Now all she would see was a man in the prime of life, dressed in a blue serge suit cut by a master hand.

And he, Fenton, had had all the bother of getting it out and having it pressed, with Fanny cursing like the devil at having her cooking interrupted.

Sir Peter had risen to his feet.

"Thank you, Fenton; and now will you be kind enough to leave us alone?" he asked.

"Very good, Sir. And shall I come and conduct Miss Hamilton back to her rooms in about an hour?"

"If you please. In exactly an hour."

Then the door was shut and Gay was alone with the tall man, who stood with his back to the fire.

As he stood there, silent, her gaze fled round

the room. A beautiful room, but desperately untidy, and even in the artificial light she could see
that it had not been properly dusted.

And the hearth. A modern, tiled hearth,
lovely golden tiles that reflected the firelight. But
oh, how it wanted tidying up! Coal and ash all
over it.

"Come nearer to me," Sir Peter said quietly.

"Not being able to use my eyes makes me
rather stupid. Where are you standing now?"

"Quite close to you."

"Do you mind if I touch you?"

"Not in the least."

Gay stood there with her eyes closed. If he
was blind, so would she be, she thought passionately.

"I shall only run my hands over your face,"
explained Sir Peter. "The fact is . . ."

And then he paused. For a wonder, he was
completely sober, he thought drily.

Had he been a little tight, he might have
been able to say what he was thinking: namely,
that he was not going to have an ugly young
woman under his roof for more than twenty-four
hours, if ample compensation and a little brutality
could get rid of her.

"Please do exactly what you like," said Gay
quietly.

"People who are blind are supposed to grow
eyes in their fingertips," said Sir Peter, "and I
think I have managed to become fairly acute in
that way."

He hesitated.

"If I may run my hands over your face, I

shall know almost exactly what you are like. Your colouring is . . . ?"

"My hair is dark and my eyes are blue," Gay told him simply.

"Thank you. That helps me. And now come along. Just a little closer. That's it."

Oh, how loudly the clock seemed to tick, thought Gay, trembling as the strong fingers took her face into their grasp.

Or was it his heart beating, the heart that was so close to her now? . . . Softly and insistently his fingers seemed to dwell on every feature.

Light as a feather and yet strong as steel.

"Thank you."

His hands had fallen to his sides.

"Thank you, that was very kind of you, Miss Hamilton."

"Not a bit."

"And now perhaps you will be kind enough to read the *Evening Standard* to me," continued Sir Peter. "You will find it on that little table close to my chair; at least that is where it ought to be."

"It is there."

"Good. Now find yourself a chair and get the light where you want it. And then read me the first page and tell me what the picture is, if there is one."

Sir Peter had sat down again and his thoughts were busy. So Fenton had lied, and lied deliberately.

This girl was young and, in her fragile, delicate way, lovely. He could tell that by the line of her chin and short, curved upper lip.

And the fringe of her lashes against her soft

young face. And the sleek cluster of her hair that nestled round her neck.

But what the devil had Fenton done it for? wondered Sir Peter, sitting there sunk low in his chair, with his penetrating and yet sightless gaze fixed on the glowing flames.

He would make Fenton as tight as a lord to-night, and keep sober himself, and get it all out of him.

* * *

It was very late indeed before Mr. Fenton began to hiccough it all out.

Sir Peter, listening, wondered how it was that he himself had been able to keep dead sober.

Somehow, as he sat there, he conceived, for one brief moment, a sickening horror of the condition into which he had allowed himself to get.

Did he, too, go on like this when he was drunk? Was he, too, maudlin and tearful and altogether repulsive?

Except for Mr. Fenton's voice, Simon's Close lay in complete silence. Even the owl that had sent its weird, penetrating hoot over the tops of the pine trees was silent.

It, too, had gone to bed, thought Sir Peter, remembering Gay's soft "Good-night" as, at his word of dismissal, she had lain down the book she was reading aloud to him and had withdrawn.

"She's lovely," said Mr. Fenton, choking, "like some beautiful flower coming out of the green grass. All pure and unspoilt and innocent."

His speech slurred more as he became more emotional.

"I could be a better man if I saw much of that lovely young thing."

"Yes."

"Such a delicate oval to her face, and her hands so sweet and small, and her soft little chin . . ."

"Yes."

"Oh, my God, why have I led the life I have?" wept Mr. Fenton. "But now it's going to be a better thing with me, indeed it is. I'll do right; all along the line I'll do right."

"Splendid," said Sir Peter drily. "Have some more brandy, Fenton?"

"Won't you join me, Sir?"

"No, thanks. I've had all I want for the moment."

"And to you, Sir. I've not been all I ought to have been to you, Sir, seeing as how you trusted me so."

Mr. Fenton walked rather uncertainly across the room to the corner cupboard.

"But that's all over. I'll be a better man."

Sir Peter's sightless gaze narrowed a little. So Fenton had been doing him, had he? Well, it served him right for leaving everything in Fenton's hands.

It had all seemed so hopeless, so impossible. And he had been ready to do almost anything to dull the ghastly despair of it.

Blind!

There was a blindness of the moral sense that was much worse than physical blindness. But if you had them both, if you didn't care a tinker's curse whether you lived or died—in fact, if you would infinitely prefer to die . . .

And what had given him this queer reaction towards his ordinary mode of life? wondered Sir Peter, as he sat, sunk low in the hide chair with its brown velvet cushions.

There was a beautiful fire and he could feel it hot on his face.

And now here came Fenton, lurching back across the room. He had helped himself to the Cointreau, and spilt it, by the smell of it.

Midnight: the clock in the corner chimed the hour musically and deliberately. Midnight. And that child under his roof, sleeping; at least he hoped she was sleeping.

"Is Miss Hamilton comfortable in her rooms, Fenton?"

"Comfortable! I've ransacked the house for the pretty creature! All the best, and I'm ashamed to think how we prepared for her, for it wasn't good enough."

He drew himself up in a pathetic effort to look dignified.

"But while she was reading to you, Sir, I did my best and so did the servants. Mrs. James, she wasn't too willing, but I saw to that," finished Mr. Fenton, smiling stupidly.

"Really!"

"I haven't done anything that you object to, Sir?"

"Not at all. I want her to be comfortable."

Sir Peter was wondering if he too should

have some brandy. That blurred feeling in his head: the only feeling worth having.

Or should he try to go to bed with nothing to drink at all and see what happened?

But he knew what would happen. He would open his eyes and stare into blackness, and then close them, and the blackness would be no more profound than it had been when they were open.

He would be tortured by his own thoughts. Forty-one years old, and perhaps another forty-one to live.

A ghastly, hideous joke of some Power Who was supposed to be beneficent.

Just because he had done what he supposed to be the thing to do, and had gone to a War that was supposed to end War.

And now they were at it again. . . . Gay's low, musical voice had read him the latest news from Abyssinia.

Did they receive the Sacraments before they brought their mechanised warfare into action?

Flying low over a collection of half-clothed natives who went to War with a few odd weapons and with their womenfolk trailing along behind them, weeping.

Could you do these things and be a follower of the Prince of Peace?

Apparently you could, thought Sir Peter sardonically.

And why was he thinking along these lines? He, who usually spent his time in cursing the Deity Who had thought fit first to create him and then to torture him.

"Time to turn in, Fenton."

He said it abruptly, for the golden smell of the brandy had become a torturing temptation.

But he would not take it tonight, he had made up his mind to it.

As some men went to the scaffold refusing to be doped, so he would go through that night without anything to drink.

"Yes, Sir."

Mr. Fenton was half-asleep. He hurriedly emptied the tumbler that he held in his hand and stood up unsteadily.

"Can I help you, Sir?" he offered.

"No, thanks," Sir Peter replied.

With a swift feeling of disgust, Sir Peter visualised the drunken ministrations of this man, who was now apparently making his way to the door.

Yes, he had knocked over a small table; books and papers were falling in a shower.

He too had knocked over a table the last time he was drunk, and with less excuse, because long practise had taught him the position of every bit of furniture in the room.

Drunk, an ugly word, that, and an ugly condition to be in!

"Good-night, Sir."

Mr. Fenton had finished picking up the papers.

"Good-night, Fenton."

Sir Peter stood alone, his sightless gaze bent towards the fire.

The fire-guard—he knew exactly where it was, and he would very soon put it in position.

But first he would flavour the utter deadliness of this lonely midnight hour. Unsleeping; he would lie in his luxurious bed unsleeping.

And towards the morning he would feel his unshaven chin, and rise with a deathly despair in his soul to face another day.

"I can't stand it."

He said the words aloud.

"And why in the name of Heaven should I? Wine to make glad the heart of man!"

He turned to thread his way carefully through the furniture to the corner cupboard.

Blind as he was, he did not fall about like that drunken fool Fenton. But then, he was not drunk, at least he was not drunk yet.

In the corridor above, Gay lay in her small bed and heard the clock strike one in the hall far below her.

Somehow it was utterly impossible to sleep. It was all too new, too exciting.

The wonderful change in her two rooms: they didn't look the same at all.

The evening with Sir Peter: reading to him, first the paper, then back to her sitting-room for dinner, and then back again to read a most interesting book about Broadmoor and those people who were to be detained during His Majesty's pleasure.

And every now and then she would lift her eyes and rest them on the tall man sunk in his chair.

'He is like a tree struck by lightning,' thought Gay. 'Blasted and greying instead of upright and full of the joy of life.'

But what had Mr. Fenton meant by saying

that there was something wrong with Sir Peter's brain? And he had been quite sober, too; at least he had seemed quite sober.

He was wonderful, thought Gay passionately. Why did she feel like this, as if he had in some way been handed over to her to take care of?

As if he were a sacred charge that she must guard as one would guard some secret document placed in one's care.

Was he asleep? wondered Gay, lying there staring at the ceiling, faintly seen in the light of the fire that was winking itself out in her sitting-room.

What must it be like to be blind so that when you closed your eyes, it was the same as when they were open?

'Lord, let him sleep,' prayed Gay fervently, and as she prayed she felt that it became somehow connected up with some vast, vibrating scheme of the universe.

"Lord, let him sleep!" she said aloud.

For if one prayed aloud, the waves of ether seized on the words and bore them off.

"Lord, let him sleep!" she again repeated.

In the room below, Sir Peter let go of the little brass latch of the corner cupboard and started to feel his way back to the fire again.

No, he would not have a drink, he decided, and would see what happened.

Half-an-hour later, he lay in his luxurious bed, with one thin hand under his face, breathing peacefully.

For almost as soon as his head had touched

the pillow, he had dropped like a stone into the profoundest depths of sleep.

Engulfed, breathing long and regularly, and lying there absolutely motionlessly under the featherweight blankets and linen sheets.

Chapter Five

During the next three weeks Fanny and George were often in consultation.

For two years they had worked at Simon's Close, and they knew every stick and stone of it.

"But such things as are happening now I never have seen," observed Fanny.

There was an amazed look about the tough lines of her square, dogged jaw.

"No, but we haven't done yet," said George. "And if she isn't careful, there'll be one of us who'll be for the high jump before she knows where she is."

"Who's that?"

"Not you or me, my girl, nor yet Elsie or Fenton. Nor the master, nor Miss Hamilton!"

"You mean Mrs. James," Fanny whispered.

George nodded.

"She'll kill him one day," he muttered.

He glanced carefully round the empty kitchen.

"She's mad with jealousy, tearing crazy with it. And Fenton's almost as bad about Miss Hamilton."

He shook his head in surprise.

"Look at the man; he's not the same at all! Got my full pay this time, I did, with no deductions for anything."

He adopted a mock superior air as he went on:

"'George, my boy,' he said, 'I've not always treated you fairly. But we've changed all that,' he said. 'From henceforth it's a square deal all round.'"

"We will now sing hymn one hundred and twenty-five," exclaimed Fanny, squalling with a sudden gust of laughter.

"That's right; that's just about the ticket. But you mind your step, my girl, or you'll find that we'll be in the soup.

"When people get like those two, there's trouble ahead. I've seen a lot of life, I can tell you, and you and I needn't keep up pretences either.

"And we've both had as much as we want of His gracious Majesty's hospitality. At least I have, speaking for myself."

"That's right," agreed Fanny solemnly.

She walked to the big range and peered professionally into a steel sauce-pan. Then as she put on the lid again she spoke thoughtfully.

"Miss Hamilton'd never look at Fenton," she said contemptuously. "She's a young lady if ever there was one! Besides, she doesn't think of anyone but the master. It's marvellous how she devotes herself to him and how she's sort of dragged him up, if you know what I mean.

"And all so dainty about it. She's the paid Secretary and she sticks to it, and never presumes as lots of young women of that age might.

"Look at what she's done, or what someone's done. Why, the grounds don't look the same even in this short time. And the central-heating started, when those corridors used to be like a living tomb!

"And Sir Peter's all smartened up about his clothes; he was always the gentleman, of course, but he used to look just ... anyhow, you know what I mean.

"Now they go walking round the garden every day, and she tells him what it's like and what's been done, and now I heard something said about a body-servant for him.

"Someone to dress him and all that; of course, it's been a disgrace the way he was allowed to go about. And that Fenton, as eager as you please about it all, and not half as much drink about as there used to be. What's it all about?"

Fanny paused wonderingly.

"Fenton was making a pretty penny up to three weeks ago, and now he doesn't seem to care about it at all."

"That's only because he's potty about Miss Hamilton," said George cheerfully. "It's wonderful what love will do, my girl. And I'm all for it so long as it doesn't go too far.

"But I don't like the look of the old girl," said George meaningfully. "And I fancy that Fenton's trying to get rid of her."

He paused dramatically.

"Well, you know how she'll take that. We all know how potty she is about him, and about that kid of theirs that you and I know all about, although they think we don't."

"Fenton's a fool; Miss Hamilton's a lady," said Fanny, "but I know what you mean, George. Anyhow, I'm all for turning over a new leaf if it means I get my pay on the right day and the right amount of it."

Fanny busied herself with the kitchen chores as she went on:

"And I'd like a kitchenmaid, if I could get a decent one, now that Elsie has such a lot of waiting to do upstairs. If this great place is going to be run as it ought to be run, we're going to need a much bigger staff than we've got now."

"That's right."

"But here you and I stick, George my boy, until we're turned out," said Fanny, grinning. "And that's not likely, because if there's one thing that I can do, it's cook."

"That's right."

"And here comes the Duchess, so mind your step."

Fanny was peering into her sauce-pan again and whispering at the same time, while George, watching Mrs. James's small black figure at the high opening of the kitchen door, wondered vaguely how it was all going to end.

'She'll swing,' he thought sombrely. 'And it'll be a pity, because she hasn't had half a chance, really.'

Then busying himself with one of the draw-

A Personal Invitation from Barbara Cartland

Dear Reader,

I have formed the Barbara Cartland "Health and Happiness Club" so that I can share with you my sensational discoveries on beauty, health, love and romance, which is both physical and spiritual.

I will communicate with you through a series of newsletters throughout the year which will serve as a forum for you to tell me what you personally have felt, and you will also be able to learn the thoughts and feelings of other members who join me in my "Search for Rainbows." I will be thrilled to know you wish to participate.

In addition, the Health and Happiness Club will make available to members only, the finest quality health and beauty care products personally selected by me.

Do please join my Health and Happiness Club. Together we will find the secrets which bring rapture and ecstasy to my heroines and point the way to true happiness.

Yours,

FREE Membership Offer

Health
&
Happiness Club

Dear Barbara,

Please enroll me as a charter member in the Barbara Cartland "Health and Happiness Club." My membership application appears on the form below (or on a plain piece of paper).

I look forward to receiving the first in a series of your newsletters and learning about your sensational discoveries on beauty, health, love and romance.

I understand that the newsletters and membership in your club are free.

* * *

Kindly send your membership application to:
Health and Happiness Club, Inc.
Two Penn Plaza
New York, N. Y. 10001

NAME_____

ADDRESS_____

CITY_____ STATE_____ ZIP_____

Allow 2 weeks for delivery of the first newsletter.

ers of the dresser, George waited for his chance to get back into his pantry again.

* * *

Those first few weeks at Simon's Close were very wonderful ones for Gay.

Her mother had written enthusiastically of Gay's new job.

"It's a great joy to us both," she wrote, "that one who is so dear to us has found her little niche in life."

And Gay, who was tidying up her bed-room before going along to read the morning paper to her employer, put the letter in her pocket, with a little smile on her soft mouth.

So they were pleased, were they? Well then, that just put the coping-stone on her happiness, for now she need not worry about her mother, who was obviously quite content.

She was free to revel in this happiness of hers!

This beautiful old house with its lovely grounds. And her rooms, most marvellously transformed by Mr. Fenton's efforts.

Her bed-room, with a beautiful satin bedspread and eiderdown to match it.

Her sitting-room, with a huge bear-skin rug in front of the fire, which was lighted every morning before she got up.

Her delicious meals—oh, how she enjoyed those! For Fanny cooked supremely well, and Fanny was a dear.

She had been down to the kitchen and had seen her. Fanny, smiling from ear to ear, and

George, in his striped galatea coat, looking sheepish.

And Mrs. James! As Gay thought of Mrs. James, she felt a little uncomfortable. Because that lady in black so obviously loathed her. Not that it mattered, for apparently she had no say in anything.

But still, the feeling that there was someone in the house who hated her gave Gay an uneasy feeling.

However, Mr. Fenton made up for it with his obvious and frantic adoration. And even that was fun, and he had certainly made everything comfortable for her.

Nobody could have been more respectful than he was. Even to have thought that he was that man who had accosted her in that field was ridiculous, thought Gay.

She looked at herself in her mirror and ruffled the waves of hair into place. For although Sir Peter could not see her, she must be just perfect in every way for him.

Also, he had now begun to ask what she was wearing, as if the sound of the colours and textures gave him pleasure.

After all, if you were blind, anything that you could visualise helped.

Gay laid down her comb and then glanced at the watch on her wrist. Ten o'clock. It was time to go along now.

Down the stairs and along the stone corridor. There was hammering going on in the hall. They were having more radiators installed.

She knocked on the heavy oak door.

"Come in."

"Good-morning, Sir Peter."

Gay's voice was light and happy as she shut the door behind her with a quick turn of her wrist.

"Good-morning."

The tall figure, standing with its back to the fire, was well groomed.

'He looks much better since I came,' thought Gay to herself, and a little flame of joy leapt up in her heart.

"How have you slept?"

"Beautifully. How have you?"

"Far better than I ever thought I should sleep unless I was tight," replied Sir Peter frankly. "I fancy there is some magic about you, my child."

"Oh."

"What's the matter?"

A quick frown drew the dark eyebrows together.

"Nothing, except that you called me 'my child,' and I love it."

She came across the room and took up *The Times* from a small table.

"Why do you love it?"

"Because it makes me feel small."

"Aren't you small?"

"No, of course I'm not."

Gay's laugh was merry.

"Feel me," she said.

She came up very close to him.

"I'll put your hand on the top of my head. I'm up to your shoulders."

"So you are, giantess!" said Sir Peter, and his stern face broke up in laughter.

"I love it when you laugh. You have only just begun to," said Gay softly.

How was it, she wondered, that she felt that she could say anything to this man whom she had only known a little under three weeks?

"It's only lately that I feel inclined to," Sir Peter pointed out, "and that is due to you, young lady.

"Now come along, and let's hear the news. *The Times* first, and then we shall know the worst.

"And after we have absorbed all that and become thoroughly depressed, we'll go out and see what they've been doing in the garden."

"That will be lovely."

"I've told Fenton to take on a couple more men."

"Oh, how splendid!"

"Yes, because as soon as Christmas is over, we shall have to get really busy in the garden."

He paused.

"What shall we do for Christmas, Miss Hamilton?"

"What do you generally do?"

"Drink myself silly," he admitted.

He moved away from the mantelpiece and began to feel his way towards the window.

"Don't begin to read yet," he said. "Come and tell me what it's like outside."

"It's grey," replied Gay promptly. "The sky is grey with little bits showing over the tops of the trees on the Woodfield Harmer side. But the whole feeling of the day is grey.

"The garden just down below the windows isn't grey, though, because the grass is marvellously green, considering the time of year."

She craned her neck slightly.

"Two men are standing down there, one with a wheel-barrow. One is the man who is always there and there is a new one.

"Now Mr. Fenton has arrived to speak to them, and he has tied a scarf round his neck because it is cold."

"I can see it all," said Sir Peter dreamily.

"I'm glad."

"Ah, that I could."

Sir Peter had moved away, his restless fingers guiding him.

Gay, looking at him, saw that his face had taken on the greyness of the day.

A feeling of impotence seized on her; what was there to say, after all?

One forgot his blindness when one was with him for long, because he disregarded it so wonderfully.

But after all, he was a blind man. If only she could think of something for him to do. If she could teach him to make something.

"Sir Peter."

"Yes?"

"I have been thinking. If only I could teach you to do something; something that might be rather a bother to learn, but would be fun."

She frowned as she thought for a few moments.

"You could learn to make model ships, or aeroplanes perhaps! Oh, I know it sounds futile,"

109

cried Gay, and her lips were trembling, "but at least it would be something. Let's try."

"Is it difficult?"

"No, no, I'm sure it's quite easy."

Her voice was eager.

"While I read, you could be doing it, and then if anything went wrong I should be there to put it right."

"Model ships!"

There was a twisted little smile on Sir Peter's sardonic mouth.

"Yes, but sailors make them," said Gay.

"In their leisure moments."

"Yes, but don't you see . . ."

"No, that's exactly what I don't," retorted Sir Peter cruelly.

He stood there, with his sightless gaze fixed on her.

This had been a mistake, he decided. For a few days he had thought that it was going to be a success.

Now that he had found out that this girl was beautiful, it had given him pleasure to feel that she was under his roof.

Decorative and young. Something fresh to divert his mind from the sickening and endless monotony of his days.

Also, there was no doubt that since her arrival he had slept a good deal better, and for that he was devoutly thankful.

But now he suddenly and abruptly craved for nothing so much as a long, unending drink. A drink that would engulf him and render him impervious to thought and feeling and everything else.

What time was it? About half-past ten or so. He would get rid of this girl and send for Fenton, and they would drink together.

She could have the day off. Yes, that was an excellent idea.

She could have the car and go to Brighton for the day, and that would please Bennett, too, for Fenton had once said something about his having a young woman at Brighton.

"How would you like to go off for the day?" he asked abruptly. "You haven't had any time off since you came, at least nothing to speak of."

His tone was brittle.

"You could take the car and go to Brighton. Get Bennett to park it, and then he could fetch you from anywhere you liked. You could go to a cinema. I believe there are several good ones in Brighton. Yes, it's an excellent idea."

Thank God, he would be free for a while. This girl had a queer effect on him. She would have to alter her ways or she would have to go.

After all, he was a free agent. If he wanted to drink, he was going to drink, and without any damned interference from anybody.

"Send Fenton to me at once," ordered Sir Peter impatiently. "I'll get him to order the car for you."

"But don't you want to go round the garden?"

"No, not today; that will do for tomorrow."

"Are you sure?"

"My dear Miss Hamilton!"

And now there was a strange, cold note in Sir Peter's voice.

"You are here as my Secretary, not as my mentor. Please do not forget it."

"I beg your pardon."

Standing there, Gay's eyes filled with tears.

'I have offended him,' she thought. 'That's what comes of being as blissfully happy as I was this morning. He doesn't really like me in the least, and the next thing will be that he'll give me notice.'

"I'll ring for Fenton," said Sir Peter.

He felt his way to the bell-push in the panelled wall.

"Now run away and get ready, and when you come back, don't disturb me. Have the evening to yourself for a change. I'll get Fenton to read me the evening paper."

Gay made no comment as he went on in that same hard voice:

"And your lunch and tea and cinema are my affair. Don't forget to tell me how much you spend. I hope you will have a very happy time."

"Thank you very much."

Dismissed, thought Gay, turning to leave the room. And something so strange and sudden about it all. They had just been about to start one of their nice mornings.

She would read *The Times* and then they would go out into the grounds, he leaning on her arm. At least, not exactly leaning, but just holding on to her so that he knew where to go.

And now ... Gay went along the corridor, feeling exactly as if she were a cat that had been cuffed on the head. All flattened ... the whole of her flattened. Snubbed.

And unconsciously she put her hands up to her small ears. Surely they were lying flat and close to her head like a cat's ears when it has been cuffed.

"Ah, Miss Hamilton."

It was Mr. Fenton, hurrying like a quick little rat towards Sir Peter's closed door.

"Sir Peter wants me, I think; he rang."

"Yes, he does," said Gay.

"After I have been in to see him, may I have a word with you?"

"Certainly."

"Thank you very much indeed."

Somehow, there was something rather consoling about the way Mr. Fenton glowed all over.

He, at any rate, liked her, thought Gay, feeling much more miserable than she had felt in some time.

This was like that tiresome game Snakes and Ladders; you got onto a square and you were all at once back at the beginning again.

She was back at the beginning, just where she had started. Dismissed as if she were a bother, when she had thought she was a comfort.

She went slowly up the staircase that led to her own corridor.

And as she went, she had a queer sensation of being watched by someone from one of the deep alcoves of the mullioned windows.

She turned to look, and stood still on the stairs. No, there was no-one. It was just her imagination; but somehow Gay felt shaken.

And yet why? She ought to be delighted to have a day off. Brighton, and going there in a beautiful car!

She would get some wool and knitting-needles there anyhow; that would make it worth-while.

Yes, there *was* someone behind her; not close behind her, but down at the bottom of the stairs along the corridor.

Gay turned again. But there was no-one, at least no-one that she could see. And what was the use of bothering about it anyway?

It would be Elsie, dusting, or George, or the new girl they had taken on to help Fanny. Not exactly a kitchenmaid, but someone to help either Mrs. James or Fanny as the case might be.

Gay went up to her rooms.

A minute or two later she heard a tap at her door.

"Come in."

"Sir Peter has told me to order the car for you, Miss."

"Yes; thank you very much."

"Would you like a foot-warmer in it?"

"Yes, I should love it," replied Gay, dimpling with sudden pleasure.

It was gratifying to be looked after like this, she thought.

"I'll get it," said Mr. Fenton.

There was something suddenly avid in his glance.

"Don't thank me. It's a joy to do anything for you, Miss."

As he came farther into the room, Gay realised that he reeked of brandy, or of some sort of spirit anyhow.

Horrid, especially at that hour of the day, thought Gay, standing there and feeling faintly disgusted.

And not only disgusted, either. Anxious! For Mr. Fenton would not have been drinking alone!

Sir Peter! He had not had anything to drink for ages, or if he had, it had not been noticeable. And now ...

That was what the Brighton plan was for, thought Gay, knowledge suddenly flooding over her. She was in the way!

Sir Peter was too well bred a man to get drunk with his lady Secretary about. But with her away in Brighton, he could drink as much as he liked and with a perfectly easy mind.

She would not go! But as she stood there, thinking this, she knew that she would have to go. She was there to do what she was told!

"Tell me if there is anything else that I can do for you, Miss."

"I don't think there is anything," said Gay easily.

And then she suddenly looked past Mr. Fenton's black-coated figure, at the door. Someone was there, lurking round the corner.

"Then I won't trouble you any further, Miss."

He turned to go.

"The car will be round at the front door in twenty minutes or so."

Mr. Fenton shut the door, and as he did so Mrs. James uttered a strangled scream.

"So you'd spy on me, would you?" Mr. Fenton said.

His impassive face had turned to flame.

Casting one quick glance up and down the deserted corridor, he clutched at the thin, convulsive throat.

Forcing the small figure down to its knees, he stood there glaring down at it.

"Let me go."

"Shall I? Or shall I finish it good and proper now?" he whispered.

And then he pushed her away from him with a brutal gesture, and Mrs. James started to run. Stumbling and running and making queer choking sounds in her throat, she moved like a hunted animal.

Along the stone corridors, down the wide staircase, and finally out of sight.

Mr. Fenton stood there trying to compose himself, and wiping his mouth with the back of his hand.

* * *

The day at Brighton was a dismal failure so far as Gay was concerned. But Bennett enjoyed it. He met her at half-past six and got neatly out of the driver's seat to open the door for her.

"I hope you have had a pleasant day, Miss," said Bennett, who liked Gay because, as he had told his girl, she was a real lady.

"Yes, thank you, Bennett," answered Gay untruthfully.

When she was in the luxurious darkness of the car, she closed her eyes with a feeling of relief.

Now that was over, and she was going home again. Home! If only she were sure that it was home for her.

Supposing Sir Peter gave her notice!

If he was tired of her, he would simply say that on reflection, her services were no longer required.

And sitting there in the darkness, Gay suddenly began to cry. Quite silently she cried, the tears streaming down her cheeks.

It was all so hopeless and disappointing! She had thought that she was in some way being a real inspiration to him and helping him to overcome the things that had dragged him down.

Helping him to take an interest in the garden and the estate. Helping him to keep his mind off the anguish of his blindness.

It was only as they turned in through the wide gates that Gay thrust her handkerchief into her pocket.

For after all, what was the use of crying? she thought dismally. Nobody cared about the tears of a hireling.

"We came along well, didn't we, Miss?"

Bennett, holding the door open, thought it was a pity that Miss Hamilton hadn't got a boy of her own.

For she was really as pretty as a picture in her three-quarter coat and little soft felt hat to match it, all so saucy with the tiny feather.

"Yes, Bennett, you drove beautifully, as you always do. Good-night, and thank you."

She passed through the front door and into the vast stone hall. It was much warmer than it used to be, noted Gay, as George shut the door and followed her into the hall.

"Shall I tell Elsie to bring up your dinner, Miss?"

"Yes, please, George."

"Mr. Fenton is not very well, Miss," he informed her. "So he's gone to bed. And if you want anything, Mrs. James will attend to you."

"Oh, thank you very much. I don't expect I shall bother her," said Gay as she went up the wide flight of stairs.

The house looked beautiful, thought Gay, with a throb of relief at being back again. Beautiful and dignified with an austere dignity of its own. If she had to leave it . . .

Gay turned the handle of her door, feeling a pang in her heart.

These lovely rooms. Someone had lit a gorgeous fire. She switched on the light. The table had all been laid so daintily. Elsie was a good girl, thought Gay, going into the inner room.

Washed and changed, she came back to the sitting-room just as Elsie arrived with the soup.

"Mr. Fenton's poorly, Miss," said Elsie importantly. "Gone to bed he has."

"Oh dear; what's the matter with him, Elsie?"

Gay drew her chair up to the table.

"Tight," replied Elsie promptly. "Roaring

tight, if you ask me! Just like he used to be a little while ago, and then he seemed to get better of it."

"Oh, Elsie!"

"And Mrs. James, she asked me to say that she won't be coming up tonight unless you want something special, as she wants to look after him."

"Yes, of course."

Sitting down at the table, she felt her heart contract. Then what about Sir Peter? Roaring drunk, too, of course.

And who was looking after him? Who was with him now, for instance?

A blind man, the worse for drink! He might fall into the fire! He might lean out the window and fall out! Did anyone care? Whose business was it?

Gay put the spoon into her soup-plate and knew that her appetite had gone.

Later, as Elsie removed the plates, she told Gay that Mrs. James would be coming to see her after all.

"About half-past nine," Elsie informed her.

"All right," said Gay agreeably.

Sunk in a low chair, she had got out her knitting. She would get on with her own jumper that she wanted to wear for Christmas.

"Good-night, Miss," said Elsie brightly, closing the door behind her.

"Good-night, Elsie."

How lovely it was to be all alone and warm, thought Gay comfortably.

Her knitting had just got to an interesting part, and it was with astonishment that she heard

119

the clock in her bed-room chime the half-hour.

Half-past what? wondered Gay, getting up to look. Half-past nine. She could hear Mrs. James coming along the corridor. Then there was a tap at the door.

"Come in."

"Good-evening, Miss Hamilton."

Mrs. James looked a little odd, thought Gay, standing there and looking at her.

"Good-evening. Do come in, Mrs. James."

"No, I can't stop. Mr. Fenton isn't very well. He'll be all right after a good night's rest, it's just his heart."

"Oh yes."

"Have you been along to see Sir Peter, Miss?"

"No," replied Gay, and her heart gave a great leap.

But he had told her not to disturb him, so of course she couldn't.

"Well, I should feel easier about him if you just went along to have a look," said Mrs. James. "Not yet, but say at about ten."

She paused before she continued:

"He doesn't like me fussing him, but you could just pop in and ask if you could read the paper to him or anything, couldn't you? Mr. Fenton generally goes, but he can't tonight."

"I see."

"And now I'll say good-night, Miss."

Her tiny figure suddenly seemed more erect than generally.

"And I hope you'll sleep well and have pleasant dreams."

Then Mrs. James was gone, leaving behind her the most extraordinary feeling of discomfort, thought Gay, shivering a little.

Yet what was it? This evening was the same as all the other evenings in this great, gaunt house. She was accustomed to being alone up in the corridor above Sir Peter's wing.

It was something about Mrs. James, of course, that gave her the feeling. It always did. There was something malignant about the little woman in the neat black frock; she had felt it as soon as she saw her.

And then why had she said that she was anxious about Sir Peter and that she, Gay, had better go along and see if he was all right?

She would love to, more than anything else. But he had said that he did not want to be disturbed.

And yet, supposing she didn't go now and something happened to him? Supposing Mrs. James had had some sort of presentiment?

Gay began to walk restlessly about the room. She would wait anyhow until ten o'clock or even later before she went. Then perhaps she might go, if she felt she could risk it.

She sat down and took up her knitting again. At ten o'clock, or perhaps a quarter-past, she would just creep along and listen outside.

If she didn't hear him, she would know that he had gone to bed and was all right, and that if he had been drunk he would be sleeping it off.

If she did hear him, she would just open the door very quietly and make some excuse about the evening paper so that she could satisfy herself that he was not burning himself to death or falling out the window!

Gay suddenly pulled herself up mentally as she thought how ridiculously her imagination worked when it had nothing better to do!

* * *

But it was half-past eleven before Gay laid down her knitting. Something had gone most awfully wrong with it and a great deal had had to be undone and knitted up again.

But now she would go along before she undressed.

She opened her door and stepped out into the corridor. Pitch dark. The household had retired, that was obvious.

Where was the switch? Gay groped her way to the top of the stairs. Yes, here it was, the golden candlelight flooded down the staircase.

She crept very softly down the stairs and along the carpeted corridor.

The first door was Sir Peter's study. Gay laid her soft face against the panels of it. If she heard anything, she would go in; if she didn't, she would go away.

Sir Peter, standing at the door of the corner cupboard, saw the door opening quite plainly.

He was drunk, of course, gloriously, rapturously drunk, more satisfactorily drunk than he had been in a long time.

And with that exquisite clarity of brain that made the sensation of blurred contentment so especially pleasing, he thought, staring at the door.

When he was really drunk, he didn't feel blind, he thought contentedly. He could see that door opening and that pretty little child standing there.

"Come in."

"Oh!"

"Come right in, as they say in America," said Sir Peter. "I am not really in a fit state to receive a lady, but that doesn't matter. Now that you're here, come in and shut the door behind you."

He began to thread his way between the tables heaped with books and papers, heading towards the door.

"I only just came . . ."

Gay backed a little, for the tall man coming towards her across the floor was very pale.

Very pale, and with bright, blazing blue eyes. They blazed in his thin face like wintry stars blaze in a cold sky.

"You only just came! But the point is that you did come!"

Sir Peter came closer to the door, and, feeling his way over the panels, he turned the key noiselessly in the lock and slipped it into his breast pocket.

If she had seen, she would begin to squeal and he would open it, after having a little fun with the foolish girl.

If she didn't squeal, she hadn't seen, and he would open it when he felt inclined, he thought, turning round again.

123

She was there; he could sense her standing there. A fragrance, a youth, a something that he had been badly needing for a long time and hadn't known it.

"I only just came to see if you would care for me to read the evening paper to you," said Gay, stammering.

For she was frightened. Sir Peter didn't look in the least like he generally did. If he was drunk, he was drunk in some peculiar and awful way.

In any event, the thing was for her to get out of the room as soon as she could and leave him to it.

He was perfectly all right and not in the least likely to fall either into the fire or out the window.

"Let us go back to the fire," suggested Sir Peter.

There was something vice-like in the way his hands caught her from behind. Slipping down from her shoulders to her elbows, he held her closely.

"Oh!"

"Why? Do you object?"

"Yes, I . . ."

Gay uttered a frightened little cry. This was appalling, she thought, and oh, how terribly he smelt of brandy!

"Please let go of me," she pleaded.

"But why?"

"I don't *like* it."

She tried to twist herself out of his grasp.

"But I do."

Over her head, his eyes blazed.

"I haven't had a woman in my arms for a very long time!"

His strong arms tightened their grip on her.

"And now that I have got my little Secretary securely locked in with me here, she surely cannot expect me to let her go again at her first squeal."

"Locked in?"

"Yes, rather. I took that precaution," said Sir Peter brightly. "Safety first, you know, although that doesn't apply to sightless men like me, because there's always someone ready to help the poor blind beggar.

"But there's a verse in the Holy Scriptures that I always like, which runs: 'We walk by faith and not by sight.'

"And in this case I walk by the exquisite scent and fragrance of you, little girl with the tip-tilted nose and soft mouth."

With a sudden twist of his powerful hands he had her close in his arms and had wrenched her face up to his.

"Please!"

Struggling, Gay had a sensation of mad terror. Locked in! What chance had she unless she could get away from him?

But of course she had every chance. Once out of his arms, she could dodge him easily.

And yet, as he held her fiercely to him, something within her shrank at the idea of dodging a blind man.

Something humiliating for him, so horribly at

her mercy. Once free from his grasp, every move he made she could go one better.

"Yes, you are beautiful."

Sir Peter was talking quietly. Holding her tightly by the wrists, he moved very slowly across the floor.

"But it's disappointing to kiss a woman who doesn't respond at all. I suppose it's because I'm drunk, little girl."

"Please do allow me to go," pleaded Gay desperately. "I feel that tomorrow you'll mind most frightfully that you've done this. Where is the key? Please do let me have it."

"God, no," said Sir Peter roughly. "Why, this is only the beginning of the whole thing.

"Look here, my child, I'll make it uncommonly worth your while. Especially as I should imagine . . . well, let's say that you are young: that sounds less crude.

"Go along in there and I'll follow you in a minute or two. Blind, I should bungle; and to valet a young and beautiful girl, hands should be skilful."

As she stood there in the vice of his hands, Gay wondered what anyone else would feel in her place.

But somehow she was quite calm. She would get away, and get away untouched: of that she was perfectly certain.

But she must leave without hurting his feelings too terribly. He was not drunk in an ordinary way at all.

She could perhaps wrench herself free, if she did it suddenly, and then dodge him. But every fibre of her rebelled at the idea of dodging him.

"If I promise you that I will stand perfectly still where I am, will you let go of me?" she asked painfully.

"Of course."

The strong fingers fell to his sides, and Gay stood there trembling.

"I feel . . ."

She took hold of his arm to steady herself.

"Hold on to me."

Sir Peter was groping for her other hand.

"I want to explain to you."

"Explain, then."

Through the mists of drink, Sir Peter's brain was clearing. What had he said? Something appalling, of course. But this child had kept her head.

He had locked the door, he realised. He slipped a finger and thumb into his breast pocket.

"Here is the key."

"I don't care about the key," said Gay violently. "And I don't mind what you said about . . . going into your room. It isn't that that fills my soul with horror and despair. It's seeing you like this."

She spread out her hands in a gesture of despair.

"You, so gorgeous and wonderful and so superbly brave! You and Mr. Fenton! You, whose name oughtn't to be mentioned in the same breath with his! You're so utterly different from him!

"And yet this drink drags you down into the

same horrible trough with him, like animals wallowing in something filthy!

"I know it's agony to be blind. It's hell, it's all the frightful things that one can't even imagine. But need you ... drink ... to get away from it?"

Gay's voice trembled with emotion.

"Can't you give it up? Can't you do something else? Oh, what else is there that you could do?" cried Gay.

She suddenly lost control of herself and broke out into wild sobbing.

"I can't, I simply can't bear it."

"Please."

"Yes, but I feel it like that," said Gay, choking. "I did the first time I saw you like that coming out of the inn! As if I wanted to stand between you and it.

"And yet what can I do? You won't take any notice of what I say, of course you won't. And I have got to stand and watch it ... killing me ... breaking my heart!"

"Come come!"

And now Sir Peter's voice was steady. He slipped his arm round her slim body.

"I am abominable," he mumbled. "I'm foul, filthy. Call me anything you like. Forgive me."

"I ... loved it when ... you ... kissed me," said Gay, sobbing. "I can't help saying so. And if it would mean that you would stop drinking, I would even ... give myself to you like that, although really I should ... wish I hadn't afterwards.

"I mean to say that it's a frightful thing for a girl to do. But if it would help you . . ."

She looked at him with tears in her eyes.

"Oh, why did I come in here tonight?" wailed Gay. "Think of the despair now. I shall never, never be happy again."

"Please don't say that."

"How can I?"

Gay was hunting wildly for her handkerchief.

"I always lose it," she explained with a ghost of a smile.

"Have mine."

"Thank you."

Burying her face in the soft silk, Gay gave one or two little hiccoughing sighs.

"Oh." The word came with a sobbing breath.

"Happier?"

"Yes, I think so." Gay laughed unsteadily.

"You don't mind my arm round you?"

"No."

Sir Peter's sightless gaze was levelled above Gay's head.

"Shall we sit down?" he asked.

"Yes; here's your chair."

"You sit in it and I will stand."

"No, you sit in it and I will kneel."

Close up to the arm of the brown leather chair, she knelt and gazed at him with her heart in her eyes.

This was love, of course, she thought simply.

Love was when you felt that you just wanted to tear your heart out of your body and hand it over to somebody else. That whatever they did was right, because it was them.

"Tell me that you have forgiven me," said Sir Peter.

"There was nothing to forgive."

"Nothing to forgive?"

"No."

"My child . . ."

Sir Peter sat very still.

"By the help of God," he said quietly, "and I shall need it, I know, I will not, *I will not*, drink to excess again."

He shuddered a little.

"The utter degradation of it."

"No, no."

"And yet you know it is."

Sir Peter smiled. "And now you must go to bed, and to sleep. Can you find your way? Is the light on? Because it is very late."

"Yes, I turned it on."

"I will unlock the door for you. Come along."

He got up out of his chair, and, stooping, he lifted her up.

"A willing prisoner this time," he said gently, and he smiled again.

"Would you kiss me again?" asked Gay simply. "Then I should feel that everything was all right again, and you were not angry with me."

"Angry with you!"

Taking her face between his hands, he turned it a little downwards and kissed her hair.

"It's parted in the middle," he said.

"Yes, it is."

"And now sleep well."

With the door wide open, he stood there towering over her. And as he closed it again he remained motionless for a moment.

And then, walking a little unsteadily across the room, he dropped down into his chair again and buried his face in his hands.

Chapter
Six

A Clergyman has a good deal to worry him,
and Mr. Clements was worried now.

He reread the Bishop's letter, over which
he had been reflecting for a good half-hour since
breakfast.

My dear Clements,

*About three weeks ago, I wrote to you
about Thornely, but I wrote a little uncertainly, as beyond what I had seen in the papers I
knew very little about him. Now I have heard
him for myself. I was on a week's holiday at
Canterbury, where he was conducting a Healing Mission, so I was able to attend the services quite unnoticed by anyone.*

*I was profoundly impressed. I went per-
fectly prepared to disapprove, for, as you
know, I have a vigorous dislike of anything
approaching emotionalism. But I came away
fully convinced that if we had more men like
Thornely in the Church, it would not be in the*

132

*condition in which it is today. I cannot speak
more forcibly than that.*

*Thornely, with whom I had a talk at the
close of the Mission, is only too glad to visit
Churches and to hold Missions in them.
But he only goes where he is invited.*

*What about consulting your Church
Council? I think that Woodfield Harmer,
with its beautiful old Church, and situated
as it is, almost midway between Brighton
and Lewes, would be ideal for a Mission.*

*In any event, think it over, and if I may
say so, pray it over.*

*Yours ever,
Chilingford*

The Vicar sighed. A Healing Mission meant a
lot of work, and the full cooperation of the
Church Council would be essential.

But if that was what the Bishop wanted, he
would support the project whole-heartedly. . . .

* * *

Gay moved about in a dazed condition of
happiness, although hers was not the happiness
of a woman who knows herself to be beloved.

No. Gay only loved, only adored. This man,
this blind man; if only she could give him her
sight!

She would, she *would*, thought Gay, pacing
about her sitting-room until it was time to go and
read to him.

She had not seen him since the night before.
That awful night when he had turned the key
in the lock. And yet, had it been awful?

When you loved, did it matter what the beloved did, so long as it was he who did it?

No; the awful part had been in seeing him drunk. Drunk—the very word was disgusting.

Oh, but how good came out of evil, thought Gay passionately. For being drunk and forgetting how to behave, he had sworn never to drink to excess again.

Yes, but would he keep that promise? People said that once a person gave way to drink, nothing would ever really cure them. That they would keep away from it for weeks, for months perhaps, and then break out again.

How would she endure it if that happened? wondered Gay.

She glanced at herself in the mirror, for although he could not see her, it was important how she looked. She knew she looked nice, in a soft new saxe-blue cardigan and skirt.

Ten o'clock: nearly time to go to Sir Peter's room; only another quarter-of-an-hour . . .

Sir Peter, who had shaved and dressed a little more carefully than usual, was speaking very seriously to Mr. Fenton.

"I want everything but the brandy taken out of that corner cupboard," he ordered.

"Don't throw it away or do anything theatrical of that kind, of course, as it may be wanted for visitors, but I have finished with this sort of thing, Fenton, and if you take my advice, you will too.

"A few nights ago we both made beasts of ourselves, and I repeated the process last night."

Sir Peter spoke slowly and deliberately.

"But I am determined, absolutely *determined*, that it shall be the last time."

"Yes, Sir."

"Have you any bills for me?"

"No, Sir."

"Are you sure? It is some time since I signed any cheques."

"Perfectly sure, Sir."

"Are we up-to-date with everything? As you know, I like the staff to be paid regularly."

"Quite up-to-date, Sir."

Sir Peter felt like retorting: "Then what the hell have you done before with all the money I've given you?"

But he remained silent as Mr. Fenton went out, quietly closing the door.

There had been some very queer cooking of accounts going on, and for a very long time, too.

But if all was square now, what did it matter? In the future everything was going to be conducted on very different lines. He would have his Lawyer down and talk it all over with him.

He hadn't seen old Paton for years and years. And, having found out from him exactly how he stood financially, he would set about altering things.

To begin with, he would have a valet of his own, so that he was certain of being properly turned out.

Then the staff must be increased, so that they could entertain. Entertain! Whom? He had not had one of his relations inside the place for years!

But now, somehow, he felt that everything must be different.

Swept and garnished, so that the disgusting, squalid, drunken life that he had led up till then could be thrust out of sight, forgotten. A humiliating thing of the past, thought Sir Peter, getting up and beginning to feel his way about the room.

That child would be coming in to read to him. His hand came into contact with the folded newspapers laid ready on a small table.

He would have to be discreet and guarded in his behaviour. She was only a child compared to him.

In her position as a paid member of his staff, it would be in the worst possible taste to have her think that she was anything else.

He had kissed her last night; at least, he had kissed her hair. He smiled grimly. But once begin that kind of thing and you never knew where it would stop.

However . . . he had himself well under control now.

"Come in."

He stood facing the opening door.

"Well, I hope you slept well," he said lightly.

"Beautifully. Did you?"

Gay stood there, slowly closing the door with her back.

Supposing she rushed across the floor and fell at his feet; what would he do? she wondered vaguely.

"No, I slept atrociously."

"Oh, I am sorry."

"Never mind, I daresay I shall sleep better

tonight," said Sir Peter cheerfully. "And I feel very fit, so that's all that matters.

"Now then, start on *The Times;* we'll hear what that monument of circumspection has to say first, shall we?"

"Yes."

Gay sat down. What had she expected? she wondered lamely. That he would tell her to come close so that he could kiss her?

Well, if she had expected it, she was going to be disappointed, she thought, slowly opening the wide sheets that George always fastened together with a patent clip.

Down in the kitchen, on the ground floor, Fanny listened to the noise that was coming along the passage, and then winked at George, who had just come in.

"At it again," she said shortly.

"The old girl?"

"Yes, that's right."

"Why can't she leave him alone?" queried George sourly. "He's turned over a new leaf, it seems to me. He gave me my back pay he'd been holding on to, and you've had all yours too!"

"That's right."

"Well then, why doesn't she keep her mouth shut?" complained George.

"Have you ever known a jealous woman to keep her mouth shut?" asked Fanny sagely. "It's jealousy that's the matter with her; that's what the noise means."

"Jealous of her grandmother!" retorted George contemptuously. "Miss Hamilton is a lady!

She'll be after the Governor if she's after anyone. She'll never look at Fenton."

* * *

Gay heard about the Mission from Elsie.

Elsie, laying the table for supper, was full of it. An aunt of hers had heard Mr. Thornely at a big Church in Streatham.

"People couldn't get in, there were so many of them," she informed Gay excitedly. "People in wheel-chairs and on crutches, and lots of children too."

"Is Mr. Thornely coming here then?"

"Yes, Miss."

"When, Elsie?"

"The end of next week. He's coming for two days. Haven't you heard about him, Miss?" asked Elsie in a surprised tone.

"Yes, vaguely," replied Gay. "But I thought he was like so many of those people who pretend to do things, and then it all comes to nothing."

"That's not a bit like Mr. Thornely," said Elsie stoutly. "Why, Aunt says that it's all as quiet as quiet."

She paused, then added dramatically:

"And when she was there, one of the people who came on crutches set them down by the altar-rail and walked to his place without them."

"Oh, Elsie!"

Gay was suddenly one great flame of eagerness.

Sir Peter, of course! Mr. Thornely might be able to cure his blindness.

"Elsie, where can I read about it?" she asked with suppressed excitement.

"I believe Mr. Fenton's got the Parish magazine. I'll get it for you, Miss."

"Gay, left alone, sat there with her hands clenched together.

Sir Peter would never believe it, of course, and he would never consent to go to Church with a crowd of other people.

But perhaps Mr. Thornely would come up to Simon's Close, if he was asked to do it as a special favour.

Elsie returned at that moment with the magazine, and as Gay read the article about the Mission her heart sank. For it stated that if anyone wished Mr. Thornely to lay his hands on them, then their name should be sent in to the Vicar of Woodfield Harmer.

Of course, Sir Peter wouldn't dream of doing anything of the kind. But he wouldn't scoff, because he was too polite, too courteous.

And yet . . . she remembered how crammed the New Testament was with miracles of healing.

"Lord, that I may receive my sight!"

Why, someone had implored for that very thing. If only she could make him just *try*, thought Gay.

It couldn't do any harm anyhow. And it might, oh, it might do good!

She was going along after supper to read him the *Evening Standard*. She would raise the subject then. She would do this before she began to read.

Sir Peter, sitting in his accustomed chair, a whimsical little smile on his face, heard her to the end.

"This must be the same thing that Fenton is so worked up about," he observed. "He wanted to read me the Parish magazine and was quite hurt when I told him that I preferred *The Times.*"

"But . . ."

"My dear child, nothing would induce me to have anything to do with any sort of Healing Mission. I don't believe in that sort of thing. In fact, I am not at all sure that I don't entirely disapprove of it."

"But Christ did nothing else but heal people."

Gay's eyes were full of tears of disappointment.

"Quite. Christ did."

"But Mr. Thornely heals *through* Christ; he doesn't do anything by his own power," urged Gay. "It's the power of God flowing through him that heals. Why shouldn't it? The Apostles could heal. Sir Peter, please, for my sake."

She got up from her chair, rushed across the little space that separated them, and fell on her knees beside him.

"My dear little girl, don't, please."

Sir Peter sat upright and his seeking hand found and rested on her bowed head.

"Please, don't distress yourself," he said gently. "You are so good and unfailing in the way you wait on me and read to me; I hate to have to say no.

"But believe me, my dear child, and when I

say this I say it for once and for all, nothing will induce me to go near the Mission that is coming to Woodfield Harmer.

"I wish them all success in their efforts, and I am perfectly prepared to let you go to as many of the services as you like, and Fenton, too.

"I am sure that Thornely is a good and sincere man, and I daresay that for those who like it, the Mission may be very beneficial. But so far as I am concerned, it may as well not be held.

"And now get up and read to me. No; first I want to tell you something."

"What?"

Gay was getting back onto her feet and wiping her eyes. Oh, that she dared take that darling hand in hers and kiss it, she thought wildly.

"Don't sound so mournful."

"No, no, it's all right."

"Next week is going to be a very busy one for me. I have sent for my Lawyer to come down."

His voice deepened as he continued:

"You have done much more than you know, little girl. I'm going to turn over a new leaf and live a different sort of life here.

"Open up the house, increase the staff, and get in touch with my relations again.

"Somehow you've given me hope. . . . I can't explain it. It's just as if a yellow fog that shut me in had been blown away by your youthful confidence in me.

"Perhaps you haven't that confidence, I don't know, but somehow I feel that you have.

"And Fenton—you've affected Fenton in the same way. From really being a bit of a rogue,

Fenton, I honestly believe, is now as straight as I'm trying to be. Well . . ."

Sir Peter held out a lean hand.

"Where are you?"

"Here."

"Well, aren't you pleased?"

"But if your relations come down, there will be no need for me."

Gay could not help crying out the words.

"Don't let's alter things, please. Oh, I know I have no right to say it, as I've only been here a little over three weeks, but it's so heavenly as it is."

She was close to tears again.

"Why do we want more servants and people to stay? Oh, why can't it stay as it is? If you want any more done for you, I could do it. I mean, I could read to you at night if you can't sleep.

"I don't know why, but I feel as if all the joy of everything will be shattered. Once people begin to come, everything will change."

Gay, charged with nervous emotion, began to pace about the room.

"Come here."

"No; I feel only like howling like a child," said Gay brokenly.

She stood there, her trembling hands locked together.

"Don't force me to the humiliation of groping round for you."

"No, no."

Instantly she ran to him.

"And now tell me that you don't mean what you say."

"I've forgotten what I did say!"

"That everything will change."

Sir Peter stood with his hands on her shoulders. God, if only he could see her, he thought, could see what her eyes held for him. Almost old enough to be her father; and a reformed drunkard and blind into the bargain.

Rich, yes, but even that had to be ascertained from old Paton. Fenton had probably been dipping heavily into things for very many years, owing to his own shameful negligence.

In any event . . . His hand pressed heavily on her.

"We don't seem to be reading the *Evening Standard*," he said in a lighter tone.

"I'll get it."

"No, wait—I want you to be happy again."

"I am! Oh, I am!"

"And you believe me when I say that nothing will change? That you will continue to be my dear little companion?"

"I believe everything you say," replied Gay simply. "How could anyone like you even say anything that wasn't true, or do anything that wasn't utterly perfect?"

"Oh, my God!"

With a little groan, Sir Peter let his hands fall from the slender shoulders.

Impulses that he had thought were completely dead within him suddenly stirred. This time a month ago, his idea of happiness was to drink himself silly! And now . . .

Again his hands lingered on her.

Gay's face was upturned. Every atom of her

longed for him to kiss her. She would make him; by the sheer force of her longing she would make him.

But by now Sir Peter had himself in hand again.

"The *Evening Standard*," he reminded her with a smile.

"Take me back to my chair, my child. Or are you too tired to read?"

"Tired? Of course I'm not tired," replied Gay bravely.

And for the first time in her life she was glad that this man could not see.

Otherwise, surely he would have seen her agony, her utter agony of disappointment because he hadn't kissed her.

* * *

There was no doubt about it, Mr. Thornely's visit to Woodfield Harmer made a tremendous stir, and the village bore itself proudly.

There was a different atmosphere everywhere. The Sunday following Mr. Thornely's departure, all three services were wonderfully attended. The Vicar was deeply encouraged, and he wondered what it was that made him feel as if the Church had been consecrated all over again.

It hung in the air like a beautiful fragrance. "Behold, I am with you always, even unto the end."

It was true: those words were true. Mr. Thornely had made the Word of God a living, vital thing.

And Gay, telling Sir Peter about it all, made

a good deal more impression on him than he allowed her to think.

"Really, it must have been remarkable," he said.

"You can't think what it was like," explained Gay. "The hush, and the frightful sadness of seeing all those ill people, and then the healing of several of them!

"It was quite—well—miraculous . . . and there was a heavenly look of joy on Mr. Thornely's face."

"Yes, he must be a very remarkable man," said Sir Peter thoughtfully.

For a second or two he passionately regretted that he had not attended the meeting. After all, it could not have done any harm, and it might . . .

He sat back in his chair and tried to imagine what it would be like to see again! To stand at the window in the darkness and see a star or two appear in the sky.

How often he had dreamt that he could see —torturing, agonisingly realistic dreams in which he had reminded himself that it was a dream and nothing more.

And now there was someone saying with such amazing reality that this time it was not a dream. Then in a tremor of joy he felt the awakening to the gradual realisation that he had been had again.

Sir Peter let his hands fall over the arms of his chair with a gesture of despair.

Gay, seeing the gesture, sat very still. He looked tired and ill, and her heart sank. All his vitality seemed suddenly to have ebbed.

He had spoken so enthusiastically of the changes that were going to take place, and now he looked as if he didn't care what happened.

Partly it was that he was missing his usual stimulant, thought Gay, suddenly terrified.

"Shall I read?" she asked.

"No, thank you. I don't feel that I can listen," replied Sir Peter wearily. "What time is it? I can't bother to get out my watch."

"Half-past nine."

"God, is that all?"

"Shall I read some more of *Brazilian Adventure?* You liked that this afternoon."

"No, thanks. I think I'll turn in and try and get some sleep while I'm so frightfully tired. Good-night, and excuse my not getting up, won't you?"

"If only I could *do* something!" said Gay desperately. "To just leave you here like this makes me feel so perfectly awful. Let me stay and read you to sleep. I believe I could, honestly I do."

"No, thank you, my child. I shall be all right. This is one of my bad days and nights."

He sighed and said slowly:

"I've felt it all day, more or less. Tomorrow I shall be better, probably, and I have my Lawyer, Paton, coming down the day after that, and that will give me something to think about."

He smiled faintly.

"So go off to sleep, my child, and don't worry about me. Good-night, my dear."

"Good-night."

She caught his outstretched hand in hers,

146

and, careless of anything but her frantic pity for him, she laid her lips on it.

"My dear child!"

"I know, but I simply can't help it," said Gay. "To think of you here . . . and then perhaps not sleeping."

She clung to his hand.

"If I could, I would give you my eyes. . . ."

"To have you feel like that helps me very much," said Sir Peter after a little pause. "But you mustn't take what I say too much to heart.

"This has been going on for years and years, you must remember, and why I feel it more acutely just now is because I have been accustomed to get drunk when I felt like this.

"Now I'm not going to, and it makes it harder at first. After a bit it will wear off, and then I shall be thankful that I've stuck with it."

"I shall think about you all night. I can't just go and leave you like this." Gay tried to control the break in her voice by talking very quickly. "Let me come back and read to you. It might send you to sleep, you never know."

"No, dear; but if I do find that it is more than I can stand, I'll come and wake you," he assured her.

"I know where you are, and I can find my way more easily in the dark than I can in the light; although why that should be, when it's all dark to me, I don't know."

"Will you faithfully, faithfully promise to come?" Gay asked.

"Yes, I will faithfully promise."

"And you won't get cold?"

And then Sir Peter did laugh out loud.

"No, I won't get cold. I have a very warm dressing-gown."

"When you laugh I feel as if a cold stone were removed from my heart," said Gay softly.

With a quiet "Good-night" she turned to leave the room.

Sir Peter, waiting for the sound of the closing door, sat very still in his chair. Dangerous, frightfully dangerous, he thought.

And yet surely a young creature like that wouldn't dream of caring for him, especially when she had constantly seen him the worse for drink.

Probably he had got to look frightfully uncared for; even Fenton had once told him that his clothes were spotted with grease marks.

At the memory of Fenton's contemptuous voice, Sir Peter gripped the leather arm of his chair.

Thank Heaven all that was over now. Fenton had taken up an attitude very different from that of the last week or so.

It was strange, he thought. It was as if a great healing wind had rushed through Simon's Close, carrying with it all the germs that had hung round the old walls for years.

How could it be explained? wondered Sir Peter, relaxing his long limbs and letting his weary eyelids fall over his sightless eyes.

Chapter Seven

It was about quarter-past one when Sir Peter decided to wake Gay and get her to read to him.

For three hours he had been stumbling round his study; first, to put on some coal, for although the central heating was on, the atmosphere was getting chill.

And then he had gone on feeling his way round the room simply for something to do.

He had tried to play a stupid game: he had mentally numbered the different bits of furniture, and as he came to them he laid a bet on whether they would be odd or even.

But at last he began to get the feeling that unless he had some sort of living companionship, he would do what he had so often contemplated doing, which was to climb out his window and end it all.

Below, the terrace was of stone; surely he could not be expected to survive a heavy crashing on stone.

At last he let himself cautiously out of his room.

The household staff slept on the ground floor and well away in a wing, but it would be most impolitic to allow them to hear him moving about.

The uneducated mind is apt to think the worst, and, what is worse, to talk about it.

So there was something stealthy and very silent in the way he opened his door and let himself out into the corridor.

He switched out the light before he opened the door, and once outside he began to feel his way along the wall.

Tall and silent in his silk dressing-gown and soft leather slippers, he went.

At the end of the corridor would come the stairs. Up to the top of the next flight, and the child's rooms were the fourth door on the right-hand side.

At the foot of the stairs he suddenly stopped dead.

Down below in the hall, one of the grand-father clocks had just chimed the quarter: quarter-past one. As he stood very still, he could hear the clock ticking.

The air of the old house was warm, with a close, shut-up warmth.

Then very slowly Sir Peter raised his head; his blindness had given him an astoundingly acute sense of hearing.

Someone, and not so far away from him, either, was breathing. Who was it?

As stealthily as a cat, he drew back into the

arched doorway of the room at the foot of the stairs.

Whoever it was would have to come down the flight of stairs that he himself had just been going to ascend, because there was no other exit from that particular corridor.

If he kept quiet enough, he or she would come, and the manner of their coming would convey to him who it was.

He flattened himself against the panels of the door and waited.

But the clock in the hall below had struck the half-hour before he grasped that whoever it was had decided to risk it and come down.

The footsteps were light and quick, and as the figure brushed by him he heard it speak.

It was muttering to itself quickly and with a sort of catch in its breath:

"My own little boy, my baby boy. If Mother does it, it will be for her baby boy."

Then the figure had passed on its way, going as noiselessly as he himself had been going.

When he was certain that it had reached the hall and would be well out of range, Sir Peter heaved himself from against the door.

Mrs. James! What on earth was she doing up here, and at this hour?

And who was the boy she was gibbering about? Had she got one?

Somehow he had never thought of enquiring; he had taken the title "Mrs. James" as one of those titles that housekeepers always take, married or not.

151

But in any event there had been something awfully weird and horrid about the whole encounter, although perhaps it had served its turn in taking his mind off himself.

He began to mount the stairs. He would not have to frighten the child; he would wake her gently, by speaking to her, and even if she was asleep, she would probably subconsciously remember that there had been something said about his calling her if he could not sleep.

But Gay was wide awake. Sitting up in bed, she wondered what had awakened her.

She leant over and switched on her light, and then, frozen with a sudden terror, she saw the door-handle turn.

Yes, there had been someone in her room, and now they were going away; or no, they were coming in.

She swallowed back the cry that had nearly escaped her.

"Don't be frightened."

Sir Peter, staring straight ahead of him, was feeling round the walls.

How tall he was in his dressing-gown, and with his hair so beautifully brushed.

"I'm wide awake."

Gay spoke in a delicious whisper of relief.

"Wait, I'll guide you. It's all right, because you can't see. I'll wait to put on my dressing-gown."

She scrambled out of bed and took hold of his hands and held them tightly in her own.

"I feel a perfect fiend to wake you, but I

haven't been to sleep at all yet and I wondered if you would read to me for half-an-hour or so."

In the bright light his face looked very haggard.

"But you didn't wake me," Gay assured him. "I was awake."

She frowned slightly.

"It is a very odd thing, but I could have sworn that someone was in my room. I awoke because of that a few minutes ago. I switched on my light. It must have been you I heard."

"Yes, that must have been it."

Sir Peter's mind instantly fled to Mrs. James.

Mrs. James hanging about up here! What for? Sir Peter suddenly felt extremely uneasy.

He had always thought of Mrs. James as an inoffensive little nonentity. But in the early hours of the morning she had been far away from her own quarters, and talking to herself into the bargain!

He would have to speak to Fenton about it. After all, he was supposed to keep an eye on the staff.

And yet, if he did speak about it, one never knew what a man like Fenton would think!

What sort of interpretation would he put on his employer's nocturnal excursions to fetch his Secretary to read to him at half-past one in the morning?

"I have my dressing-gown on now," said Gay busily, "so I'm absolutely ready to come back with you."

Her heart sang as she stood there waiting.

So she really was of some use; he did depend on her, he did, thought Gay, longing to catch hold of his hand just for the joy of touching him.

"Splendid."

Together they retraced their steps into the big room lined with books, where the fire was glowing brilliantly.

"There's a gorgeous fire."

"Yes; I hope you won't find my bed-room cold," said Sir Peter, "because that's where I want you to read to me, if you don't mind."

"To read until you see my eyes closing, and then to go back to your own room, when I hope you will be able to go to sleep again, or I shall feel more brutally selfish than I do already."

"If only you knew how glad I am that you came."

From the collar of her pale blue dressing-gown Gay's vivid face was glowing with happiness.

"Can you find your bed?" she asked.

"Yes, that's just about one thing that I can find," said Sir Peter with a smile. "Give me two minutes to settle myself into it, and then follow me, will you?"

"I will."

And for two minutes Gay stood up very close to the fire. This was Heaven, of course. Intimate and exquisite association with the man she adored.

She glanced round her: the room was lovely, warm, and smelling of smoke and leather.

She would read to him until he fell asleep.

154

Oh, that he would fall asleep, for if this were a success, he would want her again.

"All clear."

"All right."

Gay went swiftly across the room.

To see his bed-room was another excitement. All so strange in this early hour of the morning. An owl hooted eerily from the gardens below the window.

Oh, what a lovely bed-room! Huge, and with beautiful furniture and a narrow, very low bed in one corner of the room, with a sort of built-in book-case close up beside it.

Everything at his hand: books, clock, soda-water, siphon and tumbler. . . .

"Can you find a comfortable chair?"

Oh, how difficult it was to believe that the man lying in bed, his dark head on a very high pillow, was blind, thought Gay, pushing a low chair very gently towards the bed.

"Yes, thank you."

"And is the light right?"

"Perfect, thank you."

"You know, I had no business to wake you like this," said Sir Peter restlessly. "You must stay in bed late tomorrow."

"But I love to read you to sleep," replied Gay simply. "And now, what shall I read?"

"Will you begin this? *Lost Horizon*, by James Hilton. I hear it is very good."

"Yes, I should love to."

"And when you see me shut my eyes and turn over on my pillow, will you switch off the

light and go back to your own bed? And for
Heaven's sake, go to sleep at once or I shall never
forgive myself."

"I will," promised Gay.

With a long, trembling glance at the man she
adored, she began to read.

And Mrs. James, with one vicious and passionate glance at the empty place by her side,
settled herself to sleep.

So the man who had deserted her had a rival,
had he? The smooth-faced little Miss who had
gone so fervently to the Mission was no better
than she should be, was she?

She would make capital out of this discovery
of hers! She had suspected it, of course, long
since. All the changes in the house, and the promise of more, and Arthur getting all gooey about
her—that just showed what she really was.

The very next morning when she took him
his early tea, although she had said she wouldn't
take it if he slept away from her, she would tell
him, thought Mrs. James.

* * *

But Mr. Fenton didn't believe it, and said so.

"And what's more, I don't want to hear anything more about it!" he shouted. "If you choose
to go spying about the place and let your filthy
mind get to work, it's your look-out, not mine.

"If Sir Peter was wandering about the corridors at night, it was because he couldn't sleep,
and if he went to fetch Miss Hamilton, it was so
that she should read to him.

"And if you dare to say a word against that beautiful young thing, I'll have the law on you!"

Mr. Fenton drew his thin lips back from his teeth and gulped wildly at his tea.

"You . . ."

"Get *out!*" he cried, glaring furiously across the room.

And Fanny, running like a hare back to the kitchen, told George that there was the devil to pay with the old girl, and that there was no end to the things she was saying about Miss Hamilton.

"And they're all a lot of lies," said George calmly, going on swilling his tea.

"You and me aren't going to be taken in by what that old fool says, Fanny. She's mad with jealousy, that's all it is! You and I know when there's any hanky-panky going on—at least, we ought to by now."

George winked amiably over his saucer.

"And the Governor's a gentleman for all he used to be a bit free with the liquor, and he's not going to carry on with his Secretary! Nor's Miss Hamilton either; she's a lady is our Gay, and she knows her place!

"And what with all the changes that are taking place and the Lawyer coming down today and talk of a valet! By gum, as if they were going to mess it all up by what in the best circles is called a 'liaison'!"

George's tone was contemptuous.

"You and I know the Governor better than that, and he's got his head screwed on far too tight.

"And now, Fanny my girl, you put your best foot foremost. There's company today, Lawyers and what-not. Or is it tomorrow?" asked George vaguely.

"It's tomorrow," replied Fanny scornfully. "He's coming to lunch, so the old girl says, but he's to have it alone, so it's to be served in the morning-room."

She paused for a moment in the midst of her chores.

"This house run as it ought to be would be a fine place for a good girl like your Fanny.

"Give her a couple of kitchenmaids and she'd toss up a lunch and a dinner that you wouldn't beat between Lewes and London, and that's a fact," ended Fanny with a note of triumph.

"That's right."

"But we've got to get rid of the old girl or she's going to muck it up," said Fanny thoughtfully.

"Sort of gives it all a nasty taste somehow. Fenton's better than he was, but he's not much to write home about."

Her voice sharpened as she went on:

"We've had too much of that kind of thing here, and it seems a bit unhealthy somehow."

"Mission got you, too?" asked George with a grin.

"Shut up."

"You weren't there, were you?" enquired George incredulously.

"Yes, I was, Mister George," answered Fanny resolutely. "And when I saw that young man with a face like an angel, I wished I'd had the chance to see it before I made a dirty mess of my life."

She began to sob silently into her apron.

"Oh, my God!"

"Don't you jeer at me," said Fanny, choking. "I'm going to be a better woman now, with God helping me. I know it sounds a bit of a fairy-tale, taking it all into consideration, but it's true."

She sniffed loudly.

"I'm going to serve the master faithfully if he gives me the chance to stay and do it, and I think he will, unless the old girl does the dirty on me."

"We'll cook her goose," said George, "or she'll cook it herself, which is more likely, it seems to me. Look out, here she comes."

He got up quickly out of his chair. But as he stared at the apparition standing in the door-way, his jaw fell. Then the door closed again and Mrs. James was gone.

"She's off her rocker," he said slowly as he sat down again.

"So's Fenton," said Fanny shortly, mixing an egg and flour in a pudding-bowl.

"Fine look-out for us."

"We'll get through it somehow," she said, beginning to whip up the mixture with competent fury.

* * *

After an excellent lunch, followed by coffee and a glass of liqueur brandy, Mr. Paton was in a very good temper indeed.

He congratulated George, who, immaculate in livery, stood behind his chair.

"I am very glad you are pleased, Sir."

"The establishment possesses a first-class cook," observed Mr. Paton warmly.

As well as being greatly relieved at what he saw round him, the brandy had gone a very little to Mr. Paton's head.

He was an abstemious man and very rarely had anything of an alcoholic nature with his midday meal.

"I am sure that Cook will be highly gratified by what you say, Sir," said George.

Ten minutes later he burst it all out to Fanny. And Fanny, red in the face from her exertions, and noisily drinking tea, said that she was glad to hear it.

"The old girl is as nasty as she can be," she informed George. "Fenton's been up with the Governor all the morning, going through the accounts."

Fanny's voice was scornful.

"She takes it that he's in with Miss Hamilton! Lot of nonsense!"

"But we're a sure thing, old girl, and I wouldn't be surprised if they got Forrester back. That was a bit of dirty work, if you like."

"That's right."

"Wouldn't mind working under him," said George. "He was a gentleman's servant, he was."

"That's right."

"Shouldn't ever have been let go," said George, getting slowly and methodically out of his coat and hanging it over the back of a chair.

"That's right," repeated Fanny. "But things were on the crooked then, my boy. Now it's different. All that drinking's finished with, and a good job it is too."

In the corridor above, Mr. Paton was thinking exactly the same thing.

He had come down with great reluctance, for his last visit to the historic old house had been a very painful one.

Sir Peter had been unreservedly the worse for drink, and his attempts to draw his wealthy client's attention to the fact that he was being swindled right and left had only called forth a rather blasphemous response.

But now this was all a very different thing. As Mr. Paton sat and surveyed the altered demeanour of the man to whom he had now been talking for over an hour, he was amazed.

"I want Simon's Close to be kept as it ought to be," explained Sir Peter. "As I tell you, Fenton has been profoundly dishonest, and that for a good many years. But I am firmly convinced that that is all over.

"I have not signed a cheque for the last three weeks, and that means that he has been paying things out of his own pocket.

"That he ought to do so goes without saying, as he must have made many hundreds of pounds out of me, but people very often don't do what they ought," said Sir Peter, faintly smiling.

"Quite."

"Can you get hold of Forrester?" asked Sir Peter suddenly.

"You mean that charming old man who used to be butler here?"

"Yes."

"Yes, I am sure that I could," answered Mr. Paton. "When would you like him to come back? He went home after leaving here, and he has not taken another position."

"I should like him to come as soon as possible," said Sir Peter firmly. "He ought never to have been allowed to go, of course, but it's too late to say that now.

"However, if he is reinstated here, with a higher wage, it may do something to alleviate the sense of injustice that he must, naturally, have felt very strongly."

"Yes," agreed Mr. Paton quietly.

"And you say that in spite of everything, I am still financially sound?"

"You are still financially very sound," replied Mr. Paton, permitting himself a faint smile.

"Good, because I want to launch out," said Sir Peter restlessly. "I want to entertain. I should like to see some of my people, if they will overlook the past."

"I am sure they will do that," Mr. Paton assured him. "Lady Madeline was in my office last week and she spoke about you with regret, saying that she so much wished that you both could meet."

"Yes, I have behaved uncommonly badly," said Sir Peter frankly. "But there it is; it's no use lamenting what is behind one, is it, Paton?"

"Not in the least."

"And now I should rather like you to see my Secretary. I had to have someone to read to me, for it became intolerable with only Fenton about."

He raised his hand towards the fireplace.

"If you would just press the bell twice, Paton. I'm sorry to ask you to do it, but it takes me such a time to find it."

"Of course."

But as Mr. Paton got up to press the little button in the panelling, he felt a swift dismay flood over him.

So this was the cause of the transformation, was it? A young woman about!

What sort of a young woman would ally herself with Simon's Close and the queer reputation it had gained?

Mr. Paton sat down, suddenly feeling thoroughly uneasy. A young woman and the complications that would be certain to attend her.

This blind man; this extremely wealthy blind man, thought Mr. Paton, his eyes now fixed uneasily on the door.

Evidently, two rings of the bell summoned this young person from wherever she might find herself in this large and rambling old house.

"You wanted me?"

Gay opened the door very quietly and came straight in. She stood by Sir Peter's chair, waiting for him to speak.

'She has eyes for no-one but him,' thought the old Lawyer, gazing at her. 'And how lovely she is. Perhaps a good thing that he cannot see her.'

"Yes; I wanted to introduce Mr. Paton to you," said Sir Peter. "Mr. Paton is a very old and valued friend of mine, as well as my Legal Adviser."

"How do you do?"

163

"How do you do, Miss—"

Mr. Paton had got up out of his chair and was standing there, white-haired and courtly.

"Hamilton," replied Gay timidly.

"She takes excellent care of me, Paton."

"He won't let me do anything for him. If only he would," said Gay urgently. "I want him to learn to make things—models of ships, or aeroplanes, or . . ."

"Why don't you learn, Sir Peter?"

"Perhaps I will," replied Sir Peter merrily.

"I would get the things if you agreed. I should love to help you," said Gay eagerly.

And a few hours later Mr. Paton recounted it all to his wife.

It was perfectly obvious, he told her, that Miss Hamilton, who was a charming and extremely well-bred young woman, was madly in love with her blind employer.

"And he with her?"

"Impossible to tell," answered Mr. Paton, "although something has certainly altered the complexion of Simon's Close."

He wrinkled his nose.

"The last time I was there, the whole place smelt like a tap-room. You will remember how concerned I was when I came back."

"Yes, I remember very well indeed. But what's happened to everyone who was there then? Wasn't there some drunken valet-secretary who was almost insulting to you before you left?"

"He's still there."

"And approving of all this?"

"Apparently."

"And the housekeeper?"

"Still there too."

"Also approving?"

"It appears so," replied Mr. Paton slowly.

"I can't believe it," said Mrs. Paton briskly. "Old retainers don't, as a rule, take to innovations, especially when it means that they aren't making nearly so much out of it as they did."

She paused for a moment.

"Do you think that you've got to the bottom of it, Herbert?"

"No, I'm not at all sure that I have," answered Mr. Paton unexpectedly.

He sank a little lower in his chair and linked his long, clever fingers together over his watch-chain.

*　　*　　*

Christmas had come and gone.

An enchanted Christmas, frosty and sparkling, with all the tall firs in the gardens looking like spangled Christmas-trees.

"Tell me what it looks like."

Christmas Day was nearly over and Gay had been reading to her employer.

Somehow, all over the great house the day had been a happy one.

Fanny and George had remarked on it as they washed up together. No rows . . . there had been no rows at all.

Mrs. James and Mr. Fenton had talked amiably to each other, and there had even been an interchange of presents.

Just for that one day there had been peace,

165

and, surfeited with an abundance of excellent food, Fanny and George agreed that it was a thousand pities that it couldn't last.

Up in Sir Peter's sitting-room there was also peace.

They had dined together at a small table in the morning-room.

Sir Peter had made stumbling apologies beforehand: he ate carelessly, for it was so easy to get into bad habits.

Perhaps, after all, they had better stick to their usual plan of eating in their own rooms.

"What do I care how you eat?"

Gay had said it almost violently. So Sir Peter had given way, and Elsie had laid the table with an almost solemn excitement, with Mr. Fenton directing her.

Crackers, there were to be crackers; and flowers, beautiful chrysanthemums from the hothouses.

And the room must be properly warm.

Gay never forgot her first sight of the glowing warmth of that room, with her host standing there in evening-clothes. She had never seen him in the conventional black and white before.

"Oh!"

"Swept and garnished," she said, laughing. "And now tell me what you are wearing. I expect you have made the same effort as I have, as it's Christmas."

"My dress is black velvet. Not really a low dress, except a little at the back. It has a belt with a diamanté buckle to it. And tiny little sleeves."

"Come nearer so that I can just feel you."

166

As his hands wandered over her slender figure she tried to stop the thumping of her heart. When he touched her, how could she stop her heart from thumping?

"I haven't given you anything for Christmas," Sir Peter pointed out discontentedly. "I don't know why; I ought to have given my mind to it earlier."

His tone was suddenly eager.

"We'll go into Brighton one day and get something. Or London! We might go to London one day. I haven't been there for years."

"I don't feel the need of your giving me presents," said Gay simply. "Here comes Elsie. I can hear her along the corridor."

"Ah, yes." Sir Peter moved away. "Now then, where am I to sit?"

"Here."

Smiling, she sat down at the little round table.

"It all looks heavenly," she said. "And the crackers: do let's pull one now, then we can wear the hats."

"Righto!"

And Elsie, scuttling back to the kitchen, said that they were laughing like anything and that they had both got on hats. Sir Peter had one like a cardinal, and Miss Hamilton had one of those mortarboard things.

"She does look pretty," said Elsie, beaming.

"I bet she does," said George, who was disappointed because he had not been allowed to wait at the little dinner party.

But even Elsie had been told that she was

only to put things on the table and go away.

"If I think they are watching me, I make more of a mess of it than ever."

Sir Peter had said it simply, and Gay, acquiescing, prayed passionately that he had not heard the break in her voice as she replied.

For somehow tears seemed awfully near the surface now, thought Gay ruefully.

It was all so desperately pathetic. Blind; that gorgeous man, blind.

And then the way that he had said that he hoped she wouldn't mind there not being any champagne for dinner.

"I am sure I'm wiser not to risk anything," he had pointed out.

There was something infinitely pathetic in the way he had said it.

Now dinner was over and they sat very close to the fire in the upstairs sitting-room.

"Tell me what it looks like." Sir Peter said it again.

"Stars," she told him. "Heaps of stars. And the light from the house, shining on the snow, makes it look a sort of gorgeous blue.

"And the trees, they look exactly like Christmas-trees with tinsel sprinkled over them.

"The light from the hall windows is so bright that you can see tiny birds' footprints in the snow. That must be from the starlings; I have seen lots of starlings since it got so frosty."

"How can you see all this sitting by the fire?"

"I looked before dinner so that I could tell you."

"Kind little girl!"

"Kind! When if I could I would give you my eyes."

To her horror, she burst into a passion of tears.

"I'm so sorry," she said, sobbing. "I think it's because it's Christmas or something; you know, one gets so keyed up somehow. And then the feeling that you can't see it all. Oh, whatever will you think?"

"Think!"

Sir Peter turned his dark head a little on the velvet cushions.

"Think!" he said. "What do you suppose a man like me thinks when a sweet young girl like you weeps for him?"

He stretched out his arms.

"Come over here, my child, and kneel down by my chair if you will."

With a little rush she was by his side.

"That's better."

One of his strong hands was on her hair.

"That's better," he said again. "My little comforter—my abominably treated little comforter, for I had no business to wake you up the other night to read to me.

"That tired you out, of course. No wonder you cry. But don't cry, my child. Think of what your coming here has meant to me.

"Why, you've dragged me up from darkness into light, and all in less than a month. The place is transformed, or is very soon going to be transformed.

"You'll love Forrester, my old butler, who is coming back. He never ought to have gone, of course, but that's all part of the rottenness that is now a thing of the past.

"He'll get me a valet—he has dozens of relations in that line of life. He'll get together a proper staff, a thing that's been wanted here for years.

"And all this, my child, can be traced to you. Something in your youth—I don't know what it is, but whatever it is, it's done the trick. Hasn't it?"

Playfully his fingers found her chin and turned it upwards.

"I . . ."

"Well?"

"It's Christmas. Oh, do kiss me!" said Gay softly. "You did once, don't you remember?"

"Yes, I remember very well."

"Well then . . ."

"Yes, but . . ."

Sir Peter sat up in his chair. Leaning over the leather arm of it, he felt for her face and cupped it between his hands.

"You sweet little thing. Gay! The very name for you. But, my darling child, kisses between you and me are a mistake.

"To begin with, I am far too old. You need a younger man to kiss you as you ought to be kissed. In me you have only a battered, disillusioned man of over forty.

"Not very much over forty, certainly," said Sir Peter, smiling ruefully. "But battered and disillusioned and embittered all right! God, I should think I was!"

He sank back a little in his chair.

"I don't think so," said Gay.

"I know, that's part of the dearness of you. That's why that nice charwoman took you under her wing. She'd seen scores of companion-helps, she told you so. But only one that she took to as she did to you."

"Darling Norah!"

But Gay's eyes were on the face half-hidden in the velvet cushions.

"Did you hear from her this Christmas?"

"Yes."

"Splendid."

"Well?" queried Gay desperately.

After all, this was Christmas Day, she told herself frantically.

And it didn't matter what a man did; at least, he didn't lose any sort of dignity or anything by kissing somebody who asked him to.

And now that all sorts of changes were coming to Simon's Close, it might be the last chance she had.

And old retainer and a valet, and the house filled with Sir Peter's friends, because he must have heaps of them as well as lots of relations.

And she herself relegated to her proper place, namely, that of an exorbitantly paid secretary-companion.

Probably some relation would step in and say that it was nonsense her being there at all, that someone older would be much better in every way and far more suitable.

It was all coming to an *end*, thought Gay hopelessly!

Of course, any sane person would always have

known that it was far too good to last, to be as she was, almost the sole companion of a man like Sir Peter Somerset.

"Do you really want me to kiss you?"

Sir Peter spoke after a long silence.

"Me, whom you have seen drunk and behaving very badly even for a man who is not in complete possession of his senses?"

"I have forgotten all that."

"Your memory must be very short, darling."

"Darling!"

"Well, aren't you a darling?" Sir Peter smiled.

For of course he must not take her seriously, he told himself swiftly.

Girls contracted these adorations for men older than themselves, and the thing was to keep them firmly on a proper footing. Anything else . . .

And then as he reached out for her hand and held it closely between his own, he reflected that something else would be uncommonly pleasant.

Although out of the question, because he would have the acute agony of seeing her getting tired of it.

To trundle a blind man about for the rest of your life, even though he might be a blind man with plenty of money . . .

Besides, he did not care for her in that way. At least . . . Did he? Was he beginning to?

"What I should like best of anything would be to sit on the rug and lean against your knee," said Gay, clinging to his hand. "No-one will come in now, will they?"

"No, no-one."

"Well then . . ."

With a little sigh of content, Gay slid onto the rug. The fire was a gorgeous one and the hearth tiles were hot under her satin heels.

Nestling against his knee, she turned her face as his hand sought and found her curly head.

"Oh!"

"Happy?"

The firelight shone and sparkled in Sir Peter's sightless blue eyes.

"If I could purr I would."

"I feel rather the same," said Sir Peter dreamily.

As his hand caressed her soft neck, he wondered if he should risk it.

Ask her perfectly frankly if she would be his wife.

Then as he sat there, with the firelight hot on his face, he thought of the frightful toss-up it would be.

She adored him now; there was no doubt about that, for he could feel it. But would it last?

Blind, he would not be able to go about with her. Supposing the many-headed hydra of jealousy attacked him?

There would be occasions, when the first novelty of it all had worn off, when she would perhaps want to get away.

And then, would he find himself confronted with that most undignified of all situations: the elderly husband with a beautiful young wife whom he is afraid to let out of his sight, or rather vicinity?

173

No, better to leave it as it was . . .

"I love you," said Gay suddenly.

She flung herself round on her knees.

"It's you, touching my neck like that; I can't help saying it. Oh, why did you do it?" she asked, gasping. "I'm mad to have said it, and I don't mean it really. It's only . . ."

"Come come."

And now Sir Peter was really shaken. He sat up in his chair and drew her up into his arms.

"It's the fire," he said, "and it being Christmas. I had no right to caress you like that. I am afraid I rather did it on purpose because you are so sweet. Forgive me, darling."

"Forgive you for what? I don't care what you do," cried Gay passionately.

"It's true, I do love you. Why should I be ashamed to say it? It doesn't matter either, saying it to a man like you, because you know how I mean it and you wouldn't think less of me . . . or would you, perhaps?"

Gay felt a sudden agony of fear, and she drew herself stiffly away from him.

"Less of you?"

"Men do."

"Very young ones," said Sir Peter, smiling.

"Come back into my arms, my darling child, and you'll soon see that I don't think less of you. It's enchanting of you to have said it, Gay; and now I'm going to kiss you, if I may."

"If you may?"

"Well, it doesn't do to take too much for granted, does it?"

In the firelight, his mouth was very tender as he stooped his head to hers.

"My little darling, my very little darling," he said softly.

"And you won't let the people who are coming send me away from you?"

"I will not."

"And you'll let me be with you just as much and read to you just the same?"

"I will."

"Then . . ."

Gay sighed a long, trembling sigh.

"This is Heaven," she said softly. "Christmas Night, and you have kissed me, and I shall see you tomorrow, and the day after that, and the day after that."

"And the day after that," said Sir Peter, laughing.

There was a little silence as he laid his cheek against her soft hair. Should he or shouldn't he? The question tormented him as his senses spun.

And then he decided against it. No, the risk was too ghastly, too awful. Once say anything and the thing was done. . . .

"It's time for my little girl to go to bed," he said after a long pause.

"Oh, dear!"

"Shall I kiss you good-night? Will that make it more palatable?"

"Much more," said Gay emphatically.

Gay felt all her old confidence sweep over her again.

He had not thought anything of her saying

that she loved him; he didn't take it in any dreadful, shameful way that could leave her wishing that she were dead for having done such a ghastly thing.

He only thought her a child, and he took her declaration of love as the utterance of a child.

Well, it was a good thing that he did, thought Gay, trying to still the trembling of her body as his arms enclosed her.

"Hold your face up. Or would you rather I stood up and kissed you? Yes, that would be better."

Sir Peter was still holding one of her hands in his.

"Now then, you see how tall and fierce I am when I am on my feet. Come closer to me."

"Oh, do lift me up."

"Shall I?"

He smiled as he lifted her from the ground.

"Only a baby," he said, "and a baby who is up far too late. Hold up your baby's face, my darling, and let me kiss it."

Five minutes later, Gay closed the door of his study behind her, and shivered a little at the chill touch of the air in the long corridor.

Sir Peter, still standing with his back to the fire, wondered for one long, incoherent moment if he should call her back.

"No, no, no."

He said the words to himself almost furiously as he put a long forefinger inside his dress collar and wrenched it a little.

Chapter Eight

With the New Year came Forrester, clean-shaven and with the amiable urbanity of the well-fed cleric with evangelical tendencies.

"Well, Forrester, I am very glad to see you back again."

Sir Peter, standing on the sheep-skin hearth-rug, held out his hand in welcome.

"I cannot tell you, Sir . . ."

Forrester, after hunting for his handkerchief, blew his nose resonantly.

"You need not! The disgrace was that I ever allowed you to go," said Sir Peter heavily. "But things have changed since then, Forrester, and now I want you to put the house in order.

"I don't want any of the existing staff to go, as they seem to work well, but I want them added to.

"And in a week or so I think I shall get you to find me someone to valet me. Not just at once, but later on. When the weather improves, I shall be entertaining, but we can work up to all that gradually.

"Get things going as they ought to be: you know how that should be done better than I do! I think you'll find Fenton quite amenable now, for he too has improved out of all recognition."

"Yes, Sir Peter."

"I have a young lady to read to me now, Forrester. I find it an enormous help. The time seems to pass far more quickly."

"Yes, Sir."

Forrester permitted himself to smile.

"I notice a change in the room, Sir. The feminine touch, if I may say so. Flowers about, and so forth."

"Yes, she arranged the flowers. In fact, she ought to be along in a minute or two, and I should like you to see her. What is the time, Forrester?"

"Five o'clock, Sir."

"Yes, she will be along to read me the *Standard*. Ah, there she is. Come in, Gay. This is Forrester, who has come back to run my house for me."

"Oh, how lovely!"

And Gay said it with warmth, because it was lovely to think that there was going to be a man like Forrester at the head of things.

Sir Peter had no idea how urgently it was wanted, for things were queer at present. Elsie tried to tell her about the things that went on, and it was difficult not to listen to her, because it was interesting.

178

Apparently, according to Elsie, Mrs. James and Mr. Fenton did nothing but have the most frightful rows.

"There'll be bloodshed one day," Elsie told her ominously. "At least, Fanny says there will. She screams at him all the time, and she creeps about the house after him.

"Yesterday, when he came up to speak to you, Miss, I found her down by one of the linen cupboards. Sort of skulking," finished Elsie, and her eyes were large and round and frightened.

"Did you?" asked Gay carelessly, because she did not want Elsie to know that she didn't feel careless at all.

For Mr. Fenton was becoming a bother. He would waylay her on the stairs, and was constantly coming to her room on some pretext or other.

There was something about his aspect that was queer. He was perfectly respectful, but his eyes were strange: they looked hot and hungry as they devoured her!

It was as if he was consumed with a frantic adoration for her that he couldn't control!

But Gay couldn't even begin to admit that someone like Mr. Fenton was in love with her. In love! She shivered at the very idea.

The sight of Forrester was very reassuring.

He would put everything right and keep everyone in his place, which was what Simon's Close wanted.

With him there, everything that now seemed rather weird and uncomfortable would vanish.

Gay beamed with great friendliness at Forrester, and Forrester was pleased, for he had been alarmed when his master had told him that he had engaged a young lady to read to him.

But this really was a young lady, decided Forrester, treading his rather majestic way back to the servants' quarters.

* * *

It was amazing the difference that the advent of Forrester made to Simon's Close.

From being a rather bleak, ramshackle old house, it seemed to leap into warmth and light and activity.

Roaring fires were everywhere, and the paved hall reflected the leaping flames of piled logs.

Flowers everywhere, too; and a troop of charwomen, who arrived, hauled out carpets, beat them, and put them back again.

Furniture appeared in the hall: high-backed chairs and rush-seated stools, and low oak tables.

Gay, surveying it all, spoke in awe to the old butler.

"However have you done it, Forrester? Why, it doesn't look like the same house. Where have you got everything from?"

"I've known this house for very many years, Miss," he informed her benignly, "and there are rooms crammed with furniture upstairs.

"Sir Peter has never cared to have it all looking as to my mind a beautiful house like this should look, and we've often fallen out about it.

"But now he lets me have my own way

about it. He's a wonderful master to work for," added Forrester reverently.

"Yes, isn't he?" said Gay simply.

From that moment she gave her undivided allegiance to this old servant.

Forrester gave her a feeling of security. He walked through the long corridors, giving directions to the two new maids that he had obtained from somewhere, for Mr. Fenton seemed to have slunk into the background as far as management of the household was concerned.

But he still came far more often to her sitting-room than she liked.

Sometimes, on her return from reading to Sir Peter, she would find him standing there, waiting for her.

And then she would find it very difficult not to speak angrily to him, although in her heart of hearts she was rather afraid of speaking angrily.

He looked so queer. So unbalanced, with his unsteady gaze and trembling mouth.

But one day she decided to speak to Forrester about it. Meeting him in the hall, she asked him if he would mind coming up to her sitting-room for a minute or two.

"Certainly, Miss," said Forrester.

Mounting the shallow stairs with dignity and precision, he wondered what was coming.

Had the young lady got wind of the rumpus that Mrs. James was making about the way Fenton hung round her? And if so, what did she intend to do about it?

Something would have to be done, and soon,

thought Forrester drily, following Gay into her sitting-room and closing the door quietly behind him.

"Won't you sit down, Forrester?" asked Gay, and her delicate face was a little flushed.

"No, thank you, Miss," replied Forrester respectfully.

"Then I won't either," said Gay, "and I'd rather not, really, because it's easier to say what I've got to say standing up."

She paused before she went on:

"Forrester, I'm frightfully worried. It sounds so stupid, but you're so sensible and will understand. It's . . . it's . . . Mr. Fenton. He seems to me to have gone quite mad, somehow. Not violently mad, but just sort of idiotic!

"He's always in this room; I simply can't keep him out. Very often when I come back from reading to Sir Peter I find him sitting here."

She bit her lip.

"Well, it's so difficult to know what to do. I mean, if I seem to attach any importance to it, it makes it all so idiotic. There's no reason really why he shouldn't come to my room, he's perfectly respectful and all that.

"But it's just that I don't like it. There's something strange about it," said Gay restlessly.

"Yes, Miss, there is," agreed Forrester quietly. "I've noticed it too, and it mustn't go on. I'll see what I can do about it."

"Yes, but how can you?"

"I'll find a way."

"Without letting anyone know that I've said anything to you?"

"I quite hope so, Miss."

"Oh, thank you, Forrester."

Gay heaved a sigh of relief, for really and truly the whole thing had worried her much more than she had allowed herself to think.

It had given her the sort of feeling as though someone might jump out at her in the dark.

A queer feeling, not at all the sort of feeling to have in a great rambling house like Simon's Close, where the corridors were long and dimly lighted.

Certainly everything seemed much better lighted since Forrester had come, but still, even with him there were moments when it all seemed weird and rather ominous.

But now it was all going to be better, thought Gay happily.

"Oh, thank you, Forrester," she said again.

"Don't mention it, Miss."

With a brisk dignity of his own Forrester withdrew.

So quickly and quietly did he go that Gay could hardly believe that he had ever been there. But she felt so much better, having been able to tell him what was worrying her.

And now she would sit very close to her fire and do some mending until tea-time.

No chance of seeing Sir Peter until half-past five when she went to read to him.

How could she *exist* until then? thought Gay rebelliously, diving into her work-bag and drawing out a recalcitrant collection of silk stockings, all of which wanted a certain amount of repair.

Forrester went briskly along to his master's rooms.

This was the time to catch him, he decided, for it was better not to waste any more time about it. Something had got to be done, and at once. With head a little bent, he knocked on the door of Sir Peter's study.

"Come in."

And a quarter-of-an-hour later he had said all he had come to say.

Sir Peter, listening with attention, felt his heart contract uneasily. That time when he had surprised Mrs. James in the upper corridor!

He would not mention that to Forrester because of the occasion on which it had taken place, and one couldn't be too careful, even with an old servant.

But, in the light of what he was listening to now . . .

"What do you think we had better do, Forrester?"

"Get rid of Mrs. James and Mr. Fenton without delay, Sir. Otherwise, I'm afraid there will be serious trouble.

"She's tearing jealous, Sir, there's no other word for it. Watches him about the place like a cat watches a mouse. And when he comes downstairs again, she curses him something fearful."

"Do you suppose Miss Hamilton has noticed anything? Are you sure, Forrester, that Fenton is as much in her sitting-room as you think he is?"

"Positive, Sir."

"Then why . . . ?"

Sir Peter hesitated. And as he hesitated, he became conscious of a fury of jealous rage.

That child, with that bounder constantly in her room!

Why hadn't she complained? Why hadn't she said something about it?

Countenancing it until it became so flagrant that Forrester was obliged to come to him about it!

The whole thing was outrageous!

Sir Peter suddenly found that he was shaking. He must be careful or Forrester would notice.

But the old butler's eyes were on his master.

"Miss Hamilton spoke to me about it this morning, Sir," he pointed out. "She was anxious that you should not be troubled about it, so she came to me."

He paused before he continued:

"If I might make so bold, Sir, I think it would be better to keep it from the young lady that you have heard speak about it from me."

"Yes, certainly."

Sir Peter took a long, trembling breath. God, the relief! Then what had he suspected? That that innocent child was carrying on with a bounder like Fenton?

That was what it was to be blind, thought Sir Peter with sudden despair.

And he had even for one moment contemplated making her his wife!

To have her in that exquisite and intimate relationship, and to feel that every instant she was out of his sight she might be carrying on with someone else!

No, he was not cut out for that sort of thing. Horribly handicapped as he was, he would remain single to drag out his life to its bitter end.

And suddenly all the misery and despair that he had thought were banished forever flooded over him again.

"Thanks, Forrester, for telling me about it."

His voice was flat as he went on:

"Tomorrow I will explain to Fenton that with the altered arrangements that I am making, he and Mrs. James must find other occupation.

"I will make it very much worth their while, and I don't think we shall have any trouble with either of them."

"Very good, Sir."

"And will you tell Miss Hamilton that I shall not require her to read to me this evening. I am very tired and shall go to bed early."

"Can I do anything for you, Sir?"

"No, thank you, Forrester. I like to feel that you are about and in charge, but otherwise I am quite all right alone."

Sir Peter smiled somewhat pathetically.

Forrester, making his way majestically along the corridor, felt the tears rush up into his faithful old eyes.

"It's a shame, that's what it is, it's a shame," he said to himself as he went back to his well-equipped pantry.

* * *

That evening, it began to snow with a pitiless intensity.

Gay, sitting wretchedly in front of a roaring fire, thought it was all part of the silent, numbling disappointment that she had felt on being told that Sir Peter would not require her to read to him that evening.

"Is he quite well, Forrester?" she pleaded. "He always so enjoys hearing the *Evening Standard.*"

"He seems to me to be quite well, Miss," answered Forrester kindly.

He was sorry for Gay. She adored his master; that was quite plain.

And what would come of it, it was difficult to tell, for Sir Peter was not a gentleman to take a wife unless he really wanted to.

And blind as he was, he wouldn't want to, thought Forrester, tying his green apron round his solid waist.

Sir Peter was a man who'd want it all his own way, who liked to manage things himself, not one of those who liked to be trundled about like a sack of coke, thought Forrester, looking at the clock on the wall and noting that it was after five already.

If Fanny wanted to get out for the evening, she'd better go, because no-one knew what might be happening the next evening, what with Fenton and Mrs. James being given the order of the boot, and Sir Peter not wanting much for dinner.

He'd better find out first if Fanny had left everything as it should be so that Elsie, who was a handy girl, could warm it up.

'And I'll let George go, too,' thought Forrester briefly; 'then they'll get it over together, and I can wait on the master.'

A few minutes later, Forrester, in the big kitchen, gave his orders. And Fanny, who liked Forrester, was delighted.

"He can see me safe home, can our George," she said with a giggle.

"And what have you provided for the master?" enquired Forrester majestically.

"Clear soup, veal and ham pie, and cold savoury," replied Fanny promptly. "It's what he's got to like, Mr. Forrester, a cold savoury. Just a snippet of oyster and a spot of ham. He's asked for it once or twice."

"You think that Elsie can serve it up?"

"Elsie! She's as good as I am, nearly," said Fanny with a broad grin. "All I ask is that she keeps up a good fire here, because it's perishing cold outside and snowing like hell."

"Like hell?" queried Forrester blandly, for he had always liked Fanny, knowing her to be a first-rate cook, and honest into the bargain.

"Go on!" said Fanny, giggling again.

"How are things out there?"

Forrester jerked his chin in the direction of the housekeeper's room.

"Something horrid," replied Fanny laconically. "Talk about hell! It's a blacksmith's forge out there, with the sparks all over the place."

She glanced at the door before continuing in a lower voice:

"I'm getting a bit sick of it, I am; there's something unnatural about it. If you ask me, I think they're both off their rocker. Fenton balmy about Miss Gay, as if she'd look at the little worm, and Mrs. James after him like a dog . . ."

She stopped abruptly.

"Yes, quite," said Forrester majestically.

And as George shepherded Fanny down the drive, their footsteps muffled on the snow, he shook and howled with laughter.

"You went a bit far even for the old boy," he remarked.

"Well, I never said it," said Fanny indignantly.

She held up her face so that the heavy snow-flakes drifted onto it.

"I love the snow," she said. "It reminds me of when I was a little one. And I'm glad the old boy's come back to take charge, because it's what we wanted.

"And it's jolly decent of him to let us off to-night, because there's a good picture on for a change. We won't be back till pretty late, but so long as that Elsie has kept up a good fire, it doesn't matter and we'll have some good hot soup, George m'lad."

"A blessing I brought my torch," said George, hunching his overcoat up to his ears and flashing the little stream of white light onto the whiteness ahead of them.

"That's right," said Fanny, clutching at his young arm and slipping recklessly about in the silent falling snow.

*   *   *

It was only half-past nine when Gay decided to have a bath and go to bed.

After all, what else was there to do? she thought miserably, dragging back her curtains and looking at the snow as it sailed into sight, sparkling in the bright light from her window.

Heavenly, if you were happy, but horrible if you weren't, thought Gay, pulling the curtains together again and going into her bed-room to get undressed.

In any event, a bath would be delicious because the water was always boiling hot and the bath-room was beautifully equipped and warmed as well.

Back again in her pale blue dressing-gown, she felt a good deal better.

Her curly hair was bundled up inside a netted silk cap. She would sit by the fire and comb it so that the curls were in the proper place tomorrow and not all crooked from having got a little wet.

And this she did, so that when the door opened, she hardly turned because she thought it was Elsie with her hot-water bottle.

Rather later than usual, but that was very sensible of Elsie, as it would keep hot longer.

Then she stiffened!

A smell of brandy or some sort of spirit was coming in too!

"My little lovely girl."

Mr. Fenton, in dressing gown and pyjamas, was just inside the door.

He shut it and stood with his back against it.

"Get out of here!"

A blind rage seized Gay. How dare he? A

disgusting, common man like Mr. Fenton, in her room, when she was undressed!

"Get out of here!" she shouted again.

"Not yet, my little pet," whispered Mr. Fenton, advancing across the floor.

Gay, shaking with rage and fear, backed slowly away from him.

She would get something to hit him with! She did not care if she killed him.

"I'll . . . I'll . . . kill you if you . . . come near me," she cried, and stooped for a low stool.

"Then I'll die in your arms," he replied thickly.

Gay, still staring furiously at him, did not hear the slow opening of the door behind him.

But in a brief moment of gaping horror she did see a pair of blood-red hands uplifted, and hear the clanging of something metallic that fell and rolled away into a corner.

And then there was Mr. Fenton, sagging and crumpling into a heap, first sprawled across the corner of the table, and finally slipping from it and tumbling like an empty sack down onto the carpet.

"But what . . . ?"

Gay rushed to the corner of the room and picked up the thing that had clanged and then rolled away.

A bit of lead piping, frightfully heavy. But where had it come from?

Shuddering, she let it fall. There was hair sticking to it! Horrible!

She rushed out into the corridor, screaming:

"Forrester! Forrester!"

Her cries went echoing down the long corridor.

"Forrester, come up here! Someone has killed Mr. Fenton. He's dead in my room! He's dead! Forrester!"

Gay was shrieking.

"Coming, Miss."

For the first time in many years, Forrester was taking stairs two at a time.

While from the corridor below a door opened, and a tall figure emerged from it, groping with outstretched hands along the walls.

"Forrester, Gay, my God, what has happened? Forrester, what has happened? Tell me, for Heaven's sake."

Sir Peter stood there, rigid with anxiety and despair.

"It's Mr. Fenton, Sir."

Forrester had been into Gay's sitting-room and come out again.

"We'd better telephone for Dr. Pollard, Sir Peter. He's gone, I'm afraid."

"What do you mean, 'gone'?" asked Sir Peter irritably. "Gay, are you there? Tell me what's happened."

"No, don't say anything, Miss," ordered Forrester instantly. "Better not say anything. Ah, here's Mrs. James."

"Steady on now, Mrs. James," he said sternly. "We don't want any hysterics here. It's Fenton; he's ill."

"Ill? My Arthur!" cried Mrs. James shrilly.

"And pray, what's he doing up here at this time of night? Let me see him, please."

She pushed her way past the two men.

Then with shriller cries Mrs. James crouched over the lifeless figure.

"Arthur, my Arthur! Come back to me," she was howling.

Sir Peter stood there trembling.

"Forrester, before you telephone for the Doctor, come and tell me what has happened! Otherwise I shall not be responsible for my actions."

He held out his hand.

"Gay, will you come too, please, and leave Mrs. James with Mr. Fenton."

"But who killed him?" asked Gay stupidly.

"Killed him!"

"Gently, Sir Peter. Never mind that for a minute or two, Miss," said Forrester sensibly. "You come along with Sir Peter and me, there's a dear young lady."

And Forrester proceeded to lead the way downstairs again.

* * *

Dr. Pollard was equally sensible.

Yes, Fenton was undoubtedly dead, he informed them.

More than that it was not necessary for him to say at the moment, for of course the police must be informed at once.

"The police!"

Standing with his back to the fire, Sir Peter

thrust his hands into his pockets. His fingers were rigid.

"The police, Pollard! Surely not at this hour of the night! Why, it's midnight already."

"In a case of this kind, it's far better to get in touch with the police at once," said Dr. Pollard gravely. "I will remain here, of course, until they have come and gone."

"Can nobody stop that woman from howling?" asked Sir Peter furiously.

For, ever since she had seen Mr. Fenton's body, Mrs. James had continued to howl.

Faintly the howls came now, for the door of Gay's sitting-room had been shut on the living and the dead.

"Better leave her alone," advised Dr. Pollard, who had rarely felt more horribly uncomfortable than he did at that moment.

For who had struck the blow that had finished off the poor brute?

This child who sat pale and tearless in her blue dressing-gown, her small hands held out to the fire?

And yet it looked uncommonly like it. Self-defence, perhaps?

Well, sometimes one could get away with that, but not often nowadays.

"Has Forrester telephoned to the police-station?" asked Sir Peter after a little pause during which he felt that he would give his soul for a drink.

Pollard had refused one, mercifully; if he had smelt brandy, he would have drowned himself in it, he thought wildly.

Blind! Blind, in a crisis like this! That child! Had there been something in his suspicions?

Fenton, her lover? And then in a sudden revulsion of feeling she had turned on him?

"I think I hear a car."

A few minutes later Sergeant Driffield and Chief-Inspector Gaythorne from Lewes were being shown in.

The two men, after a formal greeting to Sir Peter, went off with Dr. Pollard, to the room upstairs, conducted by Forrester.

After a shivering silence, Gay spoke for the first time.

"Will they think I did it?" she asked flatly. "Because I didn't. Do you believe me?"

"Try and remember what happened, my darling."

Sir Peter's voice was urgent.

"Now, while we are quiet together, for anything you say to me will be locked in my heart forever. If you did it, tell me now and I'll get you out of it somehow."

"I didn't do it. But I didn't see who did."

Gay's lips trembled as she went on:

"The only thing I saw was red hands, like hands ... drenched ... in ... blood, waving, and then something heavy falling. And I rushed and picked up that bit of piping."

She shuddered.

"And then?"

"I rushed out into the corridor and screamed for Forrester," said Gay simply.

"How I wish they would let me dress. I feel so odd in a dressing-gown like this."

"They will soon be gone and then you can go to bed, darling," said Sir Peter tenderly.

"Yes, but when I think that they may perhaps believe I did it, I get a sort of sick feeling of terror."

She spread out her hands hopelessly.

"How can I explain it? I picked up the piping; my fingerprints will be on it, and if no-one else's are, they'll be certain it's me."

In her terror, Gay began to shiver and sob.

"Come here, my darling."

In the middle of his own awful apprehension and fear, he spoke reassuringly.

"It will only be a matter of a very few minutes now," he murmured, his lips touching her hair.

"They will ask you a few questions, of course, but you'll just answer them frankly and truthfully, and then they'll let you go to bed, my darling."

"Don't let them hang me!" cried Gay.

She clung to him desperately.

"I didn't do it, but if my fingerprints are there, they'll think that I did."

"Hush, my sweetest."

"I'm sick with fear, it's all so horrible and so awful," said Gay, sobbing. "To hear him fall on the floor; and his mouth was half-open."

"Come, come."

But as Sir Peter soothed her his face was grey. Was ever any other man in such an awful position? he wondered helplessly. Blind, useless—worse than useless.

"Don't let them take me away from you."

Gay's clutching hands were stiff with fear.

"Take you away from me! Nonsense, nonsense."

Sir Peter's sightless gaze strained over her curly head at the still-closed door.

"Why, it will be all over in a couple of minutes, my child."

"And will it be all right?"

"Perfectly all right," Sir Peter assured her, his mouth white and trembling.

* * *

But Chief-Inspector Gaythorne, although extremely kind, was adamant.

He had interviewed all the staff, he said. Two of them had just come in: George Barclay, the footman, and Fanny Morrison, the cook.

And Chief-Inspector Gaythorne, who always tried to introduce an airy note into the proceedings, which must of necessity be painful, said that the cook seemed to be more concerned that the kitchenmaid had let her fire get low than that a man was lying dead in the house.

"Indeed," said Sir Peter vaguely, who by now was almost sick with anxiety.

"It is only a matter of form," Chief-Inspector Gaythorne pointed out, "but we shall require Miss Hamilton to make a statement, so my colleague and I think it better that she should accompany us to Brighton now."

"Now!" queried Sir Peter. "But I gather that she is still in her dressing-gown."

"But why need I go?" asked Gay frantically. "I didn't do it, even if my fingerprints are on that piece of piping. I picked it up, you see, that was all."

"Don't say anything, my darling," warned Sir Peter simply.

Suddenly he felt that he didn't care if the whole world heard him. She was his darling, his baby, his sweet terrified little girl.

"Can't you come too?" Gay pleaded.

She stared, wild with fright, at the two police officials. They were so large and so unyielding.

"I tell you, I saw two blood-red hands waving in the air," she said, sobbing. "I implore you to believe me."

"That's all right, Miss," said Chief-Inspector Gaythorne reassuringly.

"You'll soon be back again, and we've got a nice rug in the car. Now you go and put on your outdoor things, and perhaps the Doctor will go along with you."

The Chief-Inspector glanced meaningly at the Doctor standing there.

* * *

How long had he sat by his dying fire? Afterwards, Sir Peter wondered.

It was still snowing. With his acutely sharpened hearing, he could almost hear the soft drifting of the flakes against his window.

It was extremely cold, but they had said that they had a rug in the car, and they were undoubtedly two kind men.

He could have gone himself, only of what earthly use would he have been?

Pollard had been very kind, too, and had

offered to stay with him, but he preferred to be alone with his despair and his agony of fear for the child he loved.

With his sight, he could have been of some practical use. He could have interviewed the servants, and cross-examined Mrs. James until in her abject fear she confessed.

But as he was, he was worse than useless!

It would be all right; of course, it would be all right.

In his extremity of fear, he kept on telling himself that it would be all right. But still . . .

Stiff and cold, he got up and began to blunder about the room. He would go mad! He would go stark, staring, raving mad. . . .

Something in his head would smash, go into splinters. He would drink . . . he would get drunk, anything to still this torment of feeling.

He would kill himself . . . it would be an easy way out of it, really . . . because one couldn't go on living, feeling like this.

Someone that you loved, in danger and in need of every atom of help and encouragement that you could give her, and he was blundering round like some great, buzzing, droning insect.

And then as a small table went flying, Sir Peter clenched his hands over his head and began to sob.

Awful tearing sobs that came up from the very depths of him. Tears that went streaming down his face.

Perhaps it was a good thing to cry: it let loose things that one could not get rid of in any other way.

In his extremity, Sir Peter went down on the floor, grovelling on his knees.

He didn't care, he didn't care what he did, no-one could see. And if they could, what did it matter?

He had led a rotten life, of course, but when one came up against it, as he was now, God was the only One left.

"Lord, that I may receive my sight!"

Someone in the Bible had said that, probably with not the faintest hope of getting what he asked for. Nor had he the faintest hope. . . .

He stumbled up from his knees again and walked to the electric-light switch.

He would have it pitch-dark and stand there by the window, with his forehead pressed against the cold glass.

"Lord, that I may receive my sight!" he repeated.

As he moved about the room, he said it aloud in a sort of quiet desperation. He had forgotten whereabouts in the room he was. Ah yes, there was the switch, and in his mind's eye he saw the sudden abrupt quenching of light.

And now here was the window; it had stopped snowing, for he could not hear that vague rustling that he had heard before.

Yes, the glass was cool. Dragging back the curtain, he laid his forehead against it.

"Lord, that I may receive my sight!"

He said it with shaking lips.

And then as he lifted his aching, swollen lids, he stood very still.

Tiny points of light ahead of him—he must

have unknowingly bumped his head against something.

Like little stars set in a black bowl. Stars!

His heart gave one great frantic leap and then seemed to stop beating. Stars!

"Lord, I believe, help Thou mine unbelief."

Not possible; no, not possible!

He lifted a shaking hand and held it level with his eyes.

Something dark now between him and the stars; some of the stars blotted out.

Ah, yes, of course, he was asleep. This was one of those hellish, tormenting dreams that he hoped he had left behind him.

Well, he would do what he always did when he had one of those tormenting dreams.

He would switch on the light so that he had the comfort of radiance all round him, although he could not see it.

Turning from the window, he let the curtain fall again, and with closed eyes groped for the switch. The table lamp, the lamp by which the child sat when she read to him.

His fingers slid up the cold stem of it.

Then, as the room leapt into sudden light, he stood very still.

Dreaming still! Then was the whole horror of this evening a dream?

He walked to the wall and pressed the little stud in the panelling. If the door opened and Forrester came in, it was not a dream. . . .

"You rang, Sir?"

Odd; he had not imagined Forrester to be nearly so old.

"Come here, Forrester."

"Yes, Sir."

"Are they back from Brighton yet?"

"Not yet, Sir."

Then it was not a dream. It was solid reality!

Instead of being a blind man, he was a man who could see!

Then what was he going to do? How was he going to behave? Yell, scream, fall on his knees and grovel in his extremity of joy?

Shout to Forrester that he could see? That he was no longer an automaton of a man who had to grope his way about and depend on the charity of others?

Fling open the windows and thrust his head out into the freezing cold and cry aloud to God in wildest thanksgiving?

No. Even when a thing like this happened, when life itself was given back to you, you had to behave as a civilised human being.

To be elemental, one had to be entirely alone with God.

And that he would be before he slept that night, thought Sir Peter, gripping his hands together and making a tremendous effort to behave normally.

"Forrester."

"Yes, Sir?"

Forrester felt that this had been a bad evening altogether, because now his master was on the verge of something or other, that was easy to see.

"Forrester, I can see you," said Sir Peter simply.

"Oh, my God, Sir, please don't," pleaded Forrester quickly. He stepped forward and dragged up a chair.

"Just here, Sir," he said, and he laid an urgent hand on Sir Peter's arm.

"But it's true, Forrester! Look, I can tell you what you are wearing. And one of your shoe-laces is untied."

"I beg your pardon, Sir, I'm sure."

Forrester was in instant confusion and stooped with a certain amount of difficulty to repair the omission.

"Oh, Forrester."

And Sir Peter stood there, his vision dimmed with tears, and he thought that, after all, why not? He was alone with an old servant.

Dropping into the chair that Forrester had brought up close to him, he buried his face in his hands.

"You're not feeling ill, Sir?"

"No, Forrester."

"How did it happen, Sir, if I may ask?" asked Forrester tremulously.

"It happened like this, Forrester," answered Sir Peter in a choked voice.

He lifted his head. And to the old servant standing there it seemed as if this master of his must have seen a vision.

'Transfigured, that's what it is, transfigured,' thought Forrester to himself as Sir Peter went on speaking.

"You see, I called upon the Lord and He heard me, Forrester, and if ever I seem likely to forget it, will you remind me of it?" he asked quietly, resting a hand on the old servant's shoulder.

Forrester, telling Fanny about it afterwards, said that he would never forget the way his master looked as he said that about having called upon the Lord.

"The Lord!" said Forrester helplessly. "And he's not a man who has ever held much to Church and its ways, either."

"The Church," retorted Fanny. "The Church isn't the Lord, although they'd like us to think so, wouldn't they?

"Although it could be if it wanted to," added Fanny thoughtfully, "if it'd shake itself up a bit and get going. Like that Mr. Thornely who came down here."

"Who's he?"

"I'll tell you tomorrow," answered Fanny wearily, "for we've had a good doing since yesterday and it's just on three o'clock now. And if this kitchen's ever to be clean again, I'll have to be up and about in a couple of hours' time."

"Well, the mess has been worthwhile," Forrester pointed out, smiling broadly.

❋ ❋ ❋

Sir Peter never forgot the scene in the great kitchen as Fanny tore the old-fashioned range to pieces.

Standing there in a mist of ash, he wondered if it were indeed he.

The faces of the servants, utterly different from anything that he had imagined.

Fanny: what a queer-looking woman!

George, sheepish and bewildered at the sight of his master moving about like an ordinary man.

"You are certain, Fanny?"

"Positive, Sir," replied Fanny. "She bought them at Brighton about a week ago. I found the bill lying about.

"Mind how you go, George, they'll fall to bits if you touch them. Ah, what's this?"

In a frenzy of excitement, Fanny was down on her knees in the hearth.

Out of a sea of ash she picked a shiny bit of red rubber shaped like a thumb.

"That's done it," she cried triumphantly.

"Pick it up with the shovel," ordered Sir Peter quickly.

How obvious it was: the blood-red hands that Gay had mentioned! India-rubber gloves, of course.

And the wearer of them must have bolted downstairs and crammed them into the range, trusting to their being burnt up at once.

And so they would have been, if Elsie had not omitted to make up the fire to Fanny's liking.

Elsie! He hadn't seen Elsie yet! Seen Elsie! Oh, God! Was it true?

"I'll take the shovel with the thumb on it just as it is," he said. "Let me know, Forrester, the moment that the Inspector is back."

"Very good, Sir."

Trembling with excitement, Forrester handed over the shovel with the incriminating fragment on it.

Then Sir Peter left the kitchen, walking firmly, with his head held high.

Left alone, the servants gaped at each other.

"It's a miracle," said Fanny after a stupefied silence. "When Forrester told me, and then the master came in after a minute or two, I could have dropped."

She paused for a moment before continuing:

"Now what's going to happen when the police come back? Although to my mind it's settled now. I bet you the old girl thought she'd settle her score with Miss Gay and get away with it!

"Huh!" she said scornfully. "She's not clever enough for that! They'll have it out of her in Brighton, or Lewes or wherever they've gone, in ten minutes or so."

"Can't we have a cup of tea?" asked George weakly.

"That we can," replied Fanny robustly.

Five minutes later, the servants sat and supped noisily at their steaming cups. It was George who lifted his pale face and nodded.

"Here they are," he said quickly.

"I'll show them straight up to the master," said Forrester.

For the next ten minutes there was silence in the big kitchen.

The clock on the wall ticked methodically and then struck the half-hour.

Elsie choked over her tea and then snuffled as Fanny spoke sharply to her.

"Hold your noise," she ordered. "We want to hear."

At last they heard steps coming rather ponderously down the wide staircase, and Forrester's subdued voice in conversation.

Then the same steps across the flagged hall, a little pause, and then the closing of the front door.

"They've gone, whoever they are," said Fanny.

And as Forrester came into the kitchen, they all three faced him breathlessly.

"Well . . . ?"

"The old girl confessed," said Forrester briefly, "and they've kept her in Lewes."

"My God!"

"Yes, it'll be the high jump for her," said Forrester with a certain amount of satisfaction. "Or detained during His Majesty's pleasure, for, if you ask me, I think she's off her rocker."

"What about the glove?"

"Inspector seemed glad to have it," replied Forrester.

"And Miss Gay?"

This time it was Elsie who had plucked up her courage to speak.

"Looks a bit tired, but that's all," said Forrester. "In ten minutes I'm to take up a cup of soup, so you get busy, Elsie my girl. Fanny's done her bit for today and she's got to get off to bed."

"Does she know the master can see?" enquired George.

"No," answered Forrester. "At least, she didn't when I left. Nor did the Inspector. He looks just the same, the master. Now then, Elsie, get busy."

*   *   *

Up in the dimly lighted study, Sir Peter stood with his back to the fire and watched the slender girl sunk in the low chair.

Far, far more beautiful than he had imagined, with an exquisite look of innocence on her young face.

While the Inspector had been there, she had not looked at him at all. Now he was waiting for her to look at him, because it was going to tell him all he wanted to know.

And as he waited, she suddenly lifted her eyes to him, sitting like that with her soft chin a little raised.

"I'm glad it's over," she murmured.

"Yes."

"I'm tired," said Gay with a sigh.

With her hands clenched together in her lap, she sat there gazing at him. With trembling chin, she tried to speak but failed.

"If . . ."

"Well?"

"I think I'll go to bed," she said falteringly.

She dropped her face into her hands and then lifted it again.

"Good-night," she said softly.

Her eyes were suddenly blinded with tears as Sir Peter saw her get up out of her chair and move towards the door.

"Gay."

"Yes."

She did not turn.

He took a quick step forward and then stood still again. No, he must have her in his arms before he told her.

"Come here," he said.

With a pathetic little cry she turned and ran to him. Clinging to him, she bowed her face on his arm. He held her to him until she had ceased to sob, then with one strong hand under her quivering chin he turned her face up to his.

"And now may I kiss you?" he asked gently.

"You know you may."

"But we'll sit in that comfortable chair for that," he said quietly. "I'll carry you to it, shall I?"

"Oh no, you might . . ."

But the warm tender lips on hers silenced her.

"I'll go very, very carefully," he whispered, lifting his head again.

"Oh, what should I do if you fell and hurt yourself?"

"But I shan't," said Sir Peter, smiling.

And somehow the exultant rapture in his voice communicated itself to Gay as she stood there encircled in his arms and gazing up at him.

"You look . . ."

Suddenly she faltered.

"How do I look?"

"Will it . . . hurt you if I . . . say it?"

"Nothing that you say to me will hurt me."

"You . . . look as if you could . . . see," whispered Gay, trembling.

"I can," said Sir Peter softly.

And as he stood there looking down into her eyes, he smiled, very tenderly.

"Peter . . . oh, Peter . . . it can't be true!"

"It is."

"Thank God . . . thank You, God . . . I've prayed and prayed . . . and now He has made . . . you see. . . ."

Gay's voice was incoherent, and then as the tears of happiness ran down her face, she said with a sob:

"I ... love ... you ... I ... love ...you so terribly ..."

"As I love you, my precious, beautiful darling," Sir Peter said.

Then there was no need for words, only kisses and more kisses which made them one.

ABOUT THE EDITOR

BARBARA CARTLAND, the celebrated romantic author, historian, playwright, lecturer, political speaker and television personality has now written over 150 books. Miss Cartland has had a number of historical books published and several biographical ones, including that of her brother, Major Ronald Cartland, who was the first Member of Parliament to be killed in the War. This book had a Foreword by Sir Winston Churchill.

In private life, Barbara Cartland, who is a Dame of the Order of St. John of Jerusalem, has fought for better conditions and salaries for Midwives and nurses. As President of the Royal College of Midwives (Hertfordshire Branch), she has been invested with the first Badge of Office ever given in Great Britain, which was subscribed to by the Midwives themselves. She has also championed the cause for old people and founded the first Romany Gypsy Camp in the world.

Barbara Cartland is deeply interested in Vitamin Therapy and is President of the British National Association for Health.

BARBARA CARTLAND
PRESENTS
THE ANCIENT WISDOM SERIES

The world's all-time bestselling author of romantic fiction, Barbara Cartland, has established herself as High Priestess of Love in its purest and most traditionally romantic form.

"We have," she says, "in the last few years thrown out the spiritual aspect of love and concentrated only on the crudest and most debased sexual side.

"Love at its highest has inspired mankind since the beginning of time. Civilization's greatest pictures, music, prose and poetry have all been written under the influence of love. This love is what we all seek despite the temptations of the sensuous, the erotic, the violent and the perversions of pornography.

"I believe that for the young and the idealistic, my novels with their pure heroines and high ideals are a guide to happiness. Only by seeking the Divine Spark which exists in every human being, can we create a future built on the foundation of faith."

Barbara Cartland is also well known for her Library of Love, classic tales of romance, written by famous authors like Elinor Glyn and Ethel M. Dell, which have been personally selected and specially adapted for today's readers by Miss Cartland.

"These novels I have selected and edited for my 'Library of Love' are all stories with which the readers can identify themselves and also be assured that right will triumph in the end. These tales elevate and activate the mind rather than debase it as so many modern stories do."

Now, in August, Bantam presents the first four novels in a new Barbara Cartland Ancient Wisdom series. The books are THE FORBIDDEN CITY by Barbara Cartland, herself; THE ROMANCE OF TWO WORLDS by Marie Corelli; THE HOUSE OF FULFILLMENT by L. Adams Beck; and BLACK LIGHT by Talbot Mundy.

"Now I am introducing something which I think is of vital importance at this moment in history. Following my own autobiographical book I SEEK THE MIRACULOUS, which Dutton is publishing in hardcover this summer, I am offering those who seek 'the world behind the world' novels which contain, besides a fascinating story, the teaching of Ancient Wisdom.

"In the snow-covered vastnesses of the Himalayas, there are lamaseries filled with manuscripts which have been kept secret for century upon century. In the depths of the tropical jungles and the arid wastes of the deserts, there are also those who know the esoteric mysteries which few can understand.

"Yet some of their precious and sacred knowledge has been revealed to writers in the past. These books I have collected, edited and offer them to those who want to look beyond this greedy, grasping, materialistic world to find their own souls.

"I believe that Love, human and divine, is the jail-breaker of that prison of selfhood which confines and confuses us . . .

"I believe that for those who have attained enlightenment, super-normal (not super-human) powers are available to those who seek them."

All Barbara Cartland's own novels and her Library of Love are available in Bantam Books, wherever paperbacks are sold. Look for her Ancient Wisdom Series to be available in August.

Barbara Cartland's Library of Love

The World's Great Stories of Romance Specially Abridged by Barbara Cartland For Today's Readers.

☐	11487	THE SEQUENCE by Elinor Glyn	$1.50
☐	11468	THE BROAD HIGHWAY by Jeffrey Farnol	$1.50
☐	10927	THE WAY OF AN EAGLE by Ethel M. Dell	$1.50
☐	10926	THE REASON WHY by Elinor Glyn	$1.50
☐	10527	THE KNAVE OF DIAMONDS by Ethel M. Dell	$1.50
☐	10506	A SAFETY MATCH by Ian Hay	$1.50
☐	11465	GREATHEART by Ethel M. Dell	$1.50
☐	11048	THE VICISSITUDES OF EVANGELINE by Elinor Glyn	$1.50
☐	11369	THE BARS OF IRON by Ethel M. Dell	$1.50
☐	11370	MAN AND MAID by Elinor Glyn	$1.50
☐	11391	THE SONS OF THE SHEIK by E. M. Hull	$1.50
☐	11376	SIX DAYS by Elinor Glyn	$1.50
☐	11467	THE GREAT MOMENT by Elinor Glyn	$1.50
☐	11560	CHARLES REX by Ethel M. Dell	$1.50
☐	11816	THE PRICE OF THINGS by Elinor Glyn	$1.50
☐	11821	TETHERSTONES by Ethel M. Dell	$1.50

Buy them at your local bookstore or use this handy coupon:

Barbara Cartland

The world's bestselling author of romantic fiction.
Her stories are always captivating tales of intrigue,
adventure and love.

☐ 11372	LOVE AND THE LOATHSOME LEOPARD	$1.50
☐ 11410	THE NAKED BATTLE	$1.50
☐ 11512	THE HELL-CAT AND THE KING	$1.50
☐ 11537	NO ESCAPE FROM LOVE	$1.50
☐ 11580	THE CASTLE MADE FOR LOVE	$1.50
☐ 11579	THE SIGN OF LOVE	$1.50
☐ 11595	THE SAINT AND THE SINNER	$1.50
☐ 11649	A FUGITIVE FROM LOVE	$1.50
☐ 11797	THE TWISTS AND TURNS OF LOVE	$1.50
☐ 11801	THE PROBLEMS OF LOVE	$1.50
☐ 11751	LOVE LEAVES AT MIDNIGHT	$1.50
☐ 11882	MAGIC OR MIRAGE	$1.50
☐ 10712	LOVE LOCKED IN	$1.50
☐ 11959	LORD RAVENSCAR'S REVENGE	$1.50
☐ 11488	THE WILD, UNWILLING WIFE	$1.50
☐ 11555	LOVE, LORDS, AND LADY-BIRDS	$1.50